"I'll be in touch," Jade said, heading for the open door. She deftly avoided shaking Carter's hand again.

As he moved up behind her, smoky desire woke in her belly, twining its way between her legs, then up through her breasts, her throat, her very fingertips. Jade quivered from the familiar longing.

Dammit. She needed to get out of this building. Fast.

"Before you leave, let's have a quick talk in my office," he rumbled in his deep voice.

Do we have to? If this were any other man, Jade would tell him where to shove his offer of a conversation. But this wasn't any man; this was Carter, and he was now a client.

She followed him, trying her best to keep her eyes at shoulder level. But with her gaze on his back, she saw clearly just how well he had filled out since college. His shoulders were so very broad and his hips narrow.

After ten years, she didn't think his presence would affect her so strongly. Her body's traitorous response triggered a hot flush of fury.

Dear Reader,

It was exciting to write the latest book in the Miami Strong series. Carter Diallo is a reliable and confident hero, always ready to solve any problem in his family's business. But Carter has one issue he hasn't been able to resolve—losing the love of Jade Tremaine when they were in college.

When Jade reappears in his life, Carter knows he's been given a second chance. But Jade will show him that forgiveness does not come easy, and he will need to work hard to win her heart.

I hope you enjoy reading Carter and Jade's story, and are inspired to always believe in love—even when the odds are stacked against you.

Best,

Lindsay

HER
PERFECT
PLEASURE

LINDSAY EVANS

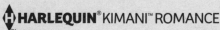

HARLEQUIN® KIMANI™ ROMANCE

Recycling programs
for this product may
not exist in your area.

ISBN-13: 978-1-335-21688-5

Her Perfect Pleasure

Copyright © 2018 by Lindsay Evans

For questions and comments about the quality of this book please contact us at CustomerService@Harlequin.com.

⊞ HARLEQUIN®
™ www.Harlequin.com

Printed in U.S.A.

Lindsay Evans was born in Jamaica and currently lives and writes in Atlanta, Georgia, where she's constantly on the hunt for inspiration, club in hand. She loves good food and romance and would happily travel to the ends of the earth for both. Find out more at www.lindsayevanswrites.com.

Books by Lindsay Evans

Harlequin Kimani Romance

Pleasure Under the Sun
Sultry Pleasure
Snowy Mountain Nights
Affair of Pleasure
Untamed Love
Bare Pleasures
The Pleasure of His Company
On-Air Passion
Her Perfect Pleasure

Visit the Author Profile page
at Harlequin.com for more titles.

For my readers.
Thank you so much for picking up my books
and continuing to read them year after year!
It means the world.

Chapter 1

Carter climbed out of the glittering turquoise pool, water dripping down his bare chest, chiseled abs, and the swimsuit clinging to his narrow hips and trunk-like thighs. The warm desert breeze brushed over him like a caress, leaving pleasurable goose bumps in its wake.

It was a damn nice day.

He ran a hand over his close-cut hair and squinted against the glare of the afternoon Las Vegas sunshine. His arms and back ached from the laps he'd swum in the Olympic-sized pool separated from the wading pool by a stylized velvet rope, and his chest rose and fell with his regulated breath.

He should've been more relaxed. Hell, he should've been a limp noodle after the fruit-heavy tropical breakfast, hour-long massage and strenuous swim he started his day with. But the dream was still riding him. Somehow, it had seemed worse than usual last night.

So instead of feeling tranquil after a long morning and afternoon of food, pampering and winning at blackjack, Carter was tense. His whole body was a mass of coiled muscle. He barely managed not to look over his shoulder, searching for a familiar pair of brown eyes, curved lips, a sweet face that begged for promises he'd never been able to keep.

At nearly three in the afternoon on a Tuesday, the hotel pool was as crowded as a Saturday night at a regular spot. But in Vegas, people didn't keep regular hours. Every night was a party. Every day was a vacation.

At his lounge chair, he scooped up his towel and roughly scrubbed it over his head, neck and chest. People watched him. Women, specifically. He could feel the burn of their eyes. Their gazes roamed his body, hard and muscled from a rigid routine in the gym, greedy and admiring.

He was used to all that and so just shrugged it off.

"Can I get you anything else, Mr. Diallo?" A poolside concierge paused by his chair, her white uniform shining in the sun while she held an empty tray at her side. She looked ready to get him just about anything he wanted.

"Just another mineral water, please."

The woman nodded and quickly flitted away to get him what he asked for.

Carter had had a whiskey sour earlier but quickly switched to water after he got a call that the reason for his Vegas trip was set to go down in just a few hours.

Alcohol never really affected him, but he didn't take the chance while he was on the job. When he was at work, he was at work.

As the head of his own security company he built from scratch, personally taking care of many of the situations his high-end clients demanded with discretion, he was always very careful to separate business from pleasure. One careless slip could mean losing everything for his client, and even for himself. Carter Diallo never slipped.

When he'd come in the day before, anticipating that the work part of his trip wouldn't start for another twenty-four hours, he took full advantage of the perks of being in Vegas. He hit a couple of the casinos, indulged in a long evening at the late-night spa before sitting down to a solitary meal in the hotel's rooftop restaurant. Views of the strip had been the ideal accompaniment to his perfectly cooked steak and creamy rosemary potatoes. He had slept well last night. Long and deep. Until the dream swept over him, that is.

A tone chimed on his phone. Three fifteen.

Carter sighed, his massive chest rising up and down with the breath.

Time for him to get to work.

"Did anyone ever tell you, blackmail isn't a very safe hobby?" Carter crossed his arms over his chest and loomed over the skinny guy cringing back in the hotel bed.

"I didn't do anything, man!"

The guy, no older than twenty-five at best, did his

best to melt into the headboard, his stupid hipster beard quivering like a weed in the storm.

When would these boys stop thinking growing big beards on their baby faces was a good substitute for actually being a man?

Carter didn't back down. He towered over the young man and deliberately used his tall and burly frame to intimidate the guy who'd dared try to blackmail his sister. His dark gray suit, worth more money than the dude could spend in a week, only added to the intimidating picture. Carter made sure of it.

"I swear, it wasn't me! Alice is lying!" The kid was trying to practically climb over the headboard and into the wall now, his skinny legs bared in some ridiculous underwear with a string that crawled between his butt cheeks.

What did Alice ever see in this guy?

"So this isn't you I see using the prepaid ATM card you demanded she send you to this post office box?" Carter showed him a picture on his cell phone.

It was undoubtedly him, despite the low-drawn hoodie and shoulders hunched away from the cameras. But the idiot wore the same shoes he'd somehow convinced Alice to buy for him, limited-edition two-thousand-dollar kicks that had only come out a few days before the photo was taken.

In the blackmail note, the kid demanded money and shoes. Greedy for everything he wouldn't get now that Alice had seen through his crap for what it was and broken up with him.

Anger boiled in Carter, a low and violent rage. But, as usual, he kept a tight grip on it, another aspect of his personality that secured him the title as the most placid Diallo brother, if also the most dangerous.

Calmly, Carter scrolled to another picture on the phone. A blown-up version of the one the boy sent to Alice's email address. In the photo, two people were obviously in an intimate situation, the boy with Alice despite what he'd amateurishly done to try and hide his face.

"Are you going to tell me this isn't you too?" Another pair of men's string underwear and expensive shoes were just within the frame.

"I'm telling you, man! I didn't do anything…" An obvious lie. The kid tried to fend Carter off with his skinny arms, but Carter wasn't about to get himself dirty by touching the little slimeball.

Instead, he growled and the kid jerked violently back into the wall, nearly giving himself a concussion. Carter held up the phone and deliberately deleted the dirty pictures of his sister though it was a mostly symbolic gesture. He'd already wiped the copies from the cloud—along with every piece of information the idiot punk stored on it—and already tracked down all the other digital and hard copies of the photos themselves. Carter darkened the phone and tucked it away in his inside jacket pocket.

Alice needed better taste in men.

"If I hear from you again *or* find out you're trying this crap with other women, I'll be back. And I won't be so nice next time."

The prepaid Visa card the kid had demanded from Alice was long empty, appearing filled with cash long enough for him to think the money—one freakin' million dollars—was there before it drained out. With his face calm and emotionless, Carter let him know that fact too.

"What? You—you can't do that!" More terrified by the loss of the money he'd stolen from Alice, he grabbed his phone, swiped and tapped the screen a few times. Carter gave him a couple of seconds to check his accounts and verify that Carter Diallo didn't make threats. Only promises.

Frantic eyes grew wider when he saw what was on the screen. "Please! I swear, I didn't mean anything by it." The phone dropped to the wrinkled sheets that smelled of sweat. Yelling and pleading, the boy grabbed for Carter's suit jacket but Carter stepped neatly back, avoiding his hands.

He was big, but fast when it counted.

"Yes, you're wiped out," Carter said. "You can move in with your mama, get a job at a fast food joint. Whatever it is, you better not try this aga—"

Just then his phone rang. It was a particular ring tone. Each of his siblings and parents had their own. It was Kingsley, his oldest brother and CEO of the Diallo Corporation calling.

"Carter," he answered although his brother obviously knew who he'd dialed.

Or at least he hoped he did. The last thing he wanted was to get another naked-butt dial from his brother who was crazy in love—and lust—with his fiancée and bride-to-be, Adah.

Kingsley, a former member of the workaholics club *except* when he escaped to Aruba once a year to windsurf or whatever, was making it work with Adah.

She lived in Atlanta and already had a business of her own there. Nothing she could easily relocate to Miami. At least not according to Kingsley. But Carter could clearly see the solution to that "problem."

"We have a situation," Kingsley said. "How soon can you get back to Miami?"

"That sounds serious."

"With the pending IPO, *everything* is serious now."

"Right." The decision to go public with their family's multibillion-dollar beauty corporation wasn't one that all the involved siblings and board members were crazy about, Carter included. But it was what most of them wanted so he'd gotten on board. "What's the problem?"

Turned out that their brother Jaxon, a local Miami celebrity and member of the corporation's board of directors, had gotten into trouble. Again. Normally it would be nothing but a blip in the Miami papers, another way for their notorious brother to impress women and get more of them into bed. But—and this was a big *but* that Carter didn't agree with and was only going along with to keep the family peace—with the pending IPO, the public scrutiny from Jaxon's increasingly stupid antics could bring ruin to the company's stock as soon as it was offered.

Carter grunted. "That damn kid..." Jaxon was eleven years younger than him.

"Yeah. I keep telling Mom to ship him off someplace—"

"Right. Like anyplace could keep him secure, much less out of trouble."

"Like I was saying..." Then Kingsley laughed, rueful and irritated at the same time. "…she basically told me the same thing you did. And I agree." They'd all like for that not to be the case, but Jaxon was his own brand of stubborn. And reckless.

"We'll deal with it. Just tell me the rest."

While his brother filled his ear with the latest problem he had to deal with as the company's "fixer," he brought up his messenger app and let his assistant know he needed an earlier flight back to Miami. By the time he had all the details of the latest Diallo disaster, he had a plane ticket already downloaded to his phone.

He'd already checked out of his hotel, figuring it would be easier to take care of business first before heading back to the Las Vegas airport.

"All right, I'll jump on the first available flight and meet you in the office." He shrugged back the sleeve of his suit jacket to glance at his watch. It was almost six. "My assistant will let you know my ETA."

"All right, sounds good." Kingsley sounded relieved.

"You just gonna stand in my hotel room all day?" the kid interrupted. The fear was leaching fast out of his little rodent-like face.

Carter knew just how to fix that. "The room is all paid up until tomorrow. But I had the receipt mailed to your house so you can know just how much you owe the Diallo family." *That's right, kid. I know where you live.* Carter tipped his head to the boy who was now visibly trembling. "Enjoy the pool here. It's no Ritz but the water is nice and warm."

He opened the door.

"Don't hang around this place too long, Trey," Carter said.

Then he closed the door behind him and headed down the stairs to the rental Benz he'd left in the nearby parking lot.

On the way to the airport in the car, he read the email Kingsley sent him about his brother's latest mess. And damn, it was a big one.

He sent Kingsley a quick message:

Not sure this is something I can handle but I'll have some ideas by the time I get there.

At the airport, he quickly made his way through the line and to his first-class seat. Ignoring the woman dressed in head-to-toe Balmain trying to get his attention with idle chatter, he scoured his brain for solutions his brother and the rest of the family could work with.

When the woman angled her immense cleavage toward him, he got an idea, reached for his phone and sent Kingsley a message.

This looks beyond my scope. If I fix this the way I want, things might backfire and blow back on the business. A buddy of mine used a firm in Cali for something similar a while back. The work was good and discreet. Here is the info to consider.

He sent the name of the firm plus his contact there just in time for the final warning from the flight attendant. He gave her his most charming smile and sat back to be a good boy.

"That's a gorgeous watch you're wearing." The woman reactivated her flirtation and stroked her long fingers along the armrest. A breath of air from the wake of her hand gave the unpleasant illusion that she'd touched him.

But he kept his hand right where it was.

"Thanks," he said. "It was a gift."

She raised a thoughtful eyebrow, obviously reevaluating him. The Tom Ford suit. Meticulous manicure. And of course, the Vacheron Constantin watch.

A faint smile twitched the corner of his mouth. He imagined that in her mind, he just went from rich boyfriend, husband or Mile High Club prospect to kept man. Or boy toy. It didn't matter what she thought, though. He wasn't interested in her right now.

Normally, he'd give maybe a tenth of his attention to flirting with a woman like her. From the faded ringfinger tan line, he could tell she was divorced. Obviously on the hunt for a new lover or husband. The sex would probably be good. Uninhibited. Maybe even a little bit kinky.

But Carter was still in work mode. Not even an impressive set of newly divorced…assets could pull his attention from where it needed to be. He'd always been a "business before pleasure" kind of guy. Even when the pleasure promised to be very pleasurable indeed.

"Whoever gave the watch to you has good taste," the woman said, her voice trailing off as obviously as her interest in Carter. No boy toy for her, then.

"Thanks." He tipped his head her way.

He wasn't like Kingsley, Jaxon or any of his brothers who had the kind of looks that made women stop in their tracks then offer up their life savings for a night or two between the sheets.

No, he wasn't as handsome as his brothers. He was, however, big and intimidating. And he was smart. The one who put his native skill set and law degree to good use to keep the family successful and thriving.

Yes, if he'd been one of his brothers, the woman would've probably still kept trying to get into his pants, figuring that although there was no money, being close to beauty like theirs for even a short time was worth any effort. But he wasn't one of the pretty ones, and that was okay.

With the woman suddenly intent on getting more champagne from the flight attendant, Carter settled down to enjoy the ride. He turned to face the window with its view of the clouds and, far away, another passenger plane flying at a lower altitude. His eyelids grew heavy. Then a familiar dream took him.

Birds chirped loud and cheerful outside his fifth-floor window and sunlight flooded into his single college room. The hard lines of a wooden chair pressed along his back, butt and thighs, and in front of him on the desk sat his half-finished homework.

Why hadn't he finished his homework yet? Class was in just a few hours.

While vague thoughts of getting back to the homework floated through his mind, his room door burst open. The most beautiful woman he had ever seen rushed through it.

Jade Tremaine. She looked like the sweet girl next door. Permed hair down to the middle of her back, a gorgeous face completely free of makeup. Her body, slender yet curvy, had a thick booty that usually starred in his juicier fantasies.

"Carter!" She was crying.

"Jade, baby, what's wrong?"

The sadness on her face carved a hole straight through Carter. If she let him, he would move the world to get rid of her tears. Her smiles made him happy. Her laughter made him laugh too. Everyone around them noticed Carter's obsession and assumed they were more than friends. But Jade already had a boyfriend, and she wasn't a cheater.

"Carter!" Jade fell into his arms, still sobbing.

This was a dream. After more than ten years of living with it, Carter knew every move he would make while trapped inside its illusion. And he knew how different it was from the real event that happened between them years ago.

Jade's slender body heaved against his.

"He cheated on me…" Her voice had wounds in it, large enough for wailing sobs to break through. "I can't believe it. I really trusted him."

Anxiety turned him inside out at the sight of her obvious pain. He would do anything to make things right for her. "Tell me," he practically begged. "Tell me what I can do."

But Jade kept sobbing on him, the same words falling from her trembling lips again and again.

"Just hold me. Please." She trembled like a leaf caught in a hurricane. "Carter…" Her body felt cool and delicate against his.

"Please, don't cry." His voice sounded hoarse and

desperate to his own ears. He needed to make everything okay for her. Carter's mind was in tatters, nothing like the logic and control that usually ruled his day-to-day life. "I'll fix whatever you want."

Slowly, the need to help her became tainted with lust and inconvenient desire. His hands wrapped around her slender arms and her skin felt like silk. "Jade, let me help you."

"Yes, yes." And she lifted her mouth toward his.

And with that, Carter knew how to help. His body and his love were what she needed.

Happiness surged in him.

Yes. This he could do.

He pressed his lips to her damp cheek and tasted her tears. A soft whimper left her parted lips and curled around his sex, hardening him. She cried out again and gripped the front of his shirt. Her sharp nails sank into his skin, deep and agonizing, but Carter moved *into* the pain.

"It'll be okay," he said. "I'll take care of everything."

"Yes," she whispered and her breath was like perfume.

They fell into his bed. A California king with sheets that brushed soft as sin against his suddenly naked skin. Carter throbbed with want to protect her and to possess her. Both impulses burned through him and scorched away every piece of reluctance he might have had before.

Her bare skin was a balm to everything that hurt; her kisses tasted of the most sacred of elixirs. With each touch of his hands on her skin, poetic nonsense invaded Carter's head. He couldn't think, could only feel.

He should stop. This wasn't right. This wasn't what she needed.

But she writhed against him, the most sensual and passionate woman he'd ever been with, "Yes, Carter..." Her tight body welcomed him. "Yes. Love me. Make everything else go away."

Yes. God, yes.

Jade panted into his open mouth. Her legs wrapped around his waist.

Her agonized sobs turned into cries of pleasure. She moaned his name. "You're perfect...Carter. So perfect." Her hand settled on his chest, over his heart, as they moved together. She threw her head back, baring her long throat. A smile curved her lips. "Yes!"

Yes, their pleasure *was* perfect.

His body moving firm and hot inside her, Carter reached for Jade's face. But his hand passed through her cheek.

Her smile fell away. "Carter?"

Suddenly, he couldn't feel her around his sex anymore. He could see her, but couldn't touch. She kept disappearing, piece after piece. "No!" she sobbed out. "Jade!"

As she disappeared around him, Carter'd never felt so helpless in his life.

He screamed out his frustration, grabbing desperately for her but his hand passed through her body again and again. He was losing everything.

Jade's sobs got louder. She trembled like she was ready to fall apart, but Carter couldn't touch her, couldn't comfort her anymore.

"Jade! Stay!"

But she didn't. Her body faded away until only her sobs lingered in the air, ripping into his ears like knives.

The jolt of the plane hitting the runway yanked Carter from the dream.

He hissed and jerked upright, opened his eyes in time to see the woman next to him give him a faintly worried glance. The pain faded. Sound drained away. But his body remained on edge and faintly aroused.

Just like always.

Ten years of having the dream and it was still as powerful as ever. The panic and regret that came with it were things he could happily live without. But he didn't know how to get rid of the dream, or those feelings.

A deep breath in. A deep breath out.

Okay. Enough of this. His body still felt heavy and in need of sleep, but that was too bad. He had work to do.

Carter's phone vibrated when he turned it on. A single message from Kingsley had come in during the five-hour flight.

Got in touch with the firm you suggested. We got lucky they took our call outside office hours. Their chief strategist will be in my office when you get here.

His brother didn't waste any time…

Other than that, only one new business emergency had come up. Plus, an update from Kingsley's fiancée about the engagement party the whole family was expected to attend. He sent his assistant the details so she could keep him on track.

As soon as the aircraft door opened and he was free to go, Carter nodded to his neighbor and left with his single piece of carry-on luggage. The patience to wait for bags to arrive at the luggage carousal just wasn't in him. Not to mention, he wasn't often anywhere long enough to need more than a change of clothes, his laptop and cell phone.

He wound his way through the airport to the curbside. A scant three minutes later, a black town car pulled up and the driver slid down the passenger-side window.

"Mr. Diallo?"

He nodded and barely moved toward the car before the driver leaped out, a woman in a crisp dark uniform, and opened the door for him.

"Thank you," he said, but she was already back in the driver's seat and pulling away from the curb.

During the drive, he checked his messages again. His assistant, who was worth her weight in gold and rubies, scheduled the meeting with Kingsley in the early afternoon. This gave Carter enough time to head home, shower, change and take care of some urgent business for his own firm. The situation with Jaxon was urgent but no one was about to keel over.

While he took care of these basic things, the chauffeur waited.

They made good time to the office and Carter offered the woman a tip, which she respectfully refused before driving away from the thirty-story Miami highrise that housed the Diallo Corporation and a few other interests the family owned.

When he walked into the building, it felt like home.

More so than the three-thousand-square-foot house he'd recently bought on Hibiscus Island.

He'd been coming to the building since he was a kid, always eager to see what magical things the lab came up with or find out firsthand what kept his parents away from home so much. Now that he knew the ins and outs of the business that kept five of the thirteen Diallo siblings employed, he half wished he hadn't been so eager to throw his childhood away just to satisfy his curiosity.

His parents had taken that curiosity for interest in running the family business, and once it had been established that he had no interest in arm wrestling the title and pain in the butt of being CEO away from Kingsley, they'd slotted him into the next best or possibly worst job. Company fixer aka CSO, chief security officer. A title he was convinced they'd made up.

It didn't matter to them that he already had his own security firm, his own employees. They were Jamaican. For them, it was perfectly normal, even expected, to have more than one job.

The elevator doors chimed and slid open.

Carter took it to the top floor and walked into his brother's office after knocking once and waiting a few seconds past the "Come in." He'd accidentally barged into enough sex-at-the-office scenarios by various members of his family with their significant others to last him a lifetime.

"You work fast, Kingsley." He closed the door behind him with a click.

God, he was tired. But sleep would have to wait.

"We don't have time to waste." Kingsley greeted

Carter with a grin despite the seriousness of what they needed to discuss. After a few quick keystrokes, Kingsley stood up and hugged Carter, gave him the manly slap on the back.

"Trust me. I understand," Carter said.

He was so focused on his brother that he didn't notice the other figure in the large office until he caught movement from the corner of his eye.

Right. The head of the California-based PR firm. Damn, he must have been more tired than he thought.

Carter turned with his hand held out to shake. "Carter Diallo," he said automatically, expecting a middle-aged white man. But he froze as a slender hand clasped his.

"We've already met," the PR chief said in a particularly expressionless voice. The corners of a familiar pair of lips curved up in a humorless smile. "Jade Tremaine, in case you've forgotten."

Chapter 2

Carter Diallo was huge.

His shoulders easily filled the doorway of his brother's office, and his presence was immense and intimidating. The impression of overwhelming strength was only made even more so by his expressionless face. He looked more like an enforcer than the CSO Jade knew he was. Thick muscles were apparent even under the sleek Tom Ford suit; his hair was perfectly and precisely cut—he was the very embodiment of class and power.

His face was still the same, though. At least his eyes were: that peculiar mix of hyperconfidence and authority that hadn't seemed to match the slender boy Jade knew in college but now seemed perfect for the giant who just walked through Kingsley Diallo's door.

No, this wasn't the man she knew in college. His effect on her equilibrium was worse. She swallowed and barreled ahead on the course she'd chosen when she first found out they would be doing business together.

"Jade Tremaine, in case you've forgotten," she said, carefully shielding her emotions from him.

His eyebrow, dark and perfectly sculpted, rose as he clasped her hand in a perfectly respectable handshake.

For such a muscled, hypermacho-looking man, he was incredibly well-groomed. His brows manicured, skin smooth and exfoliated. She couldn't remember if that was all natural or if he took as much care with his looks as she did with hers.

Looking at him, her nerves jangled all over the place. Although she'd prepared herself for Carter Diallo, just seeing him in the flesh after ten years obliterated everything from her memory except the taste of his lips.

She'd seen Carter's last name on everything, from the first email contact to the massive sign and logo on top of the building his family owned, even the transfer of her agency's fee in their account. But somehow she'd thought—hoped!—it was all a coincidence.

Until Carter walked in the door, older and even more gorgeous than ever.

She hated herself for noticing.

Kingsley had a large glassed-in office. Anyone inside could see out but no one could see in. So she saw Carter coming in from the elevator, watched him exchange a few words with Kingsley's assistant before striding with a confident, bow-legged stride toward the door. Though she'd been in the middle of a conversation with the older Diallo, Jade had turned away, flustered, to root around in her briefcase on some pretense or other. When Carter came in, he didn't see her face right away. She made sure of it.

And now...

"Not at all," he said in response to her ridiculous statement, and she immediately saw his brother take note, a shifting of the expression on his face.

But, ever the professional that Jade had known him to be in the few hours they'd known each other, Kingsley said nothing.

Carter unbuttoned his suit jacket and took a seat at the oval conference table at the far end of the spacious office like he was the one who'd called the meeting. In a way, he had, she supposed.

"Did Kingsley tell you what this is about?" He glanced briefly at his brother which was Kingsley's cue to join him at the table, apparently.

Kingsley gestured toward a seat at the table and waited for Jade to sit down before sinking into one of the sinfully comfortable leather chairs.

"Yes, he gave me the details." She put the folder she'd pulled from her briefcase on the table and tapped it with a long mocha-lacquered fingernail. "Your little brother hasn't been acting in the best interests of the company lately. His behavior *will* negatively impact the IPO offering." Jade pulled a few key sheets of paper from the folder and passed them to the two men. "Here's all the information I put together on him."

When Corrie, her assistant and the one handling the day-to-day workings of the firm while she was in Miami, called her and said Diallo Corporation was looking for a professional fixer, she'd been shocked. But jumped on it right away. Diallo was big business and it was only luck—bad or good, she wasn't sure yet—that had her in Miami this week.

Her parents' sudden deaths in a car accident yanked her from the safety and distance of her San Diego home back to Miami where she'd been mostly miserable. Or too ignorant to realize she'd been miserable. She hadn't talked to her parents in years and although her first impulse was to hand everything over to a professional to deal with, Corrie had cornered her the afternoon after she found out about the accident and basically guilted her into jumping on a plane.

Jade arrived in Miami in time for the meticulously planned funeral—her parents had been so thorough with their own arrangements, she'd hardly had to do anything—and hadn't been at all surprised by the service's sparse attendance. The ten or so people gathered around the caskets seemed more intent on avoiding each other's eyes than mourning Isaac and Abigail Tremaine.

Jade included.

Resentment was too strong a word for what she felt for her parents. It had mostly been apathy, especially after the way they'd treated her when she was in college. Even with Corrie bullying her, Jade didn't want to deal with her parents' funeral, their estate, the murky pool of unsorted emotion in her chest. She didn't want to deal with any of it.

So, it had been a blessing, she thought, when she got the call about the Diallo Corporation's interest. Sitting in front of the lawyer and painfully discussing her parents' last wishes, she'd practically jumped for joy when her cell phone rang. Now she wasn't so sure if any of this could be called a blessing.

With her escape from the lawyer's office at the forefront of her mind, she'd done the quick research on the problem—boy genius Jaxon Diallo's general tactlessness and extremely bad taste in women—printed the information she thought she would need for the quickly arranged meeting and just shown up.

Now she wasn't sure what was worse. Dealing with the lawyer telling her that her parents had always wished for her to forgive them and return home, or facing the man who'd shattered her heart into a million pieces ten years ago.

A tough choice.

"Damn, I wish Jaxon would learn a little more discretion," Kingsley said, dragging Jade's mind back from the past. "Pillow talk doesn't have to include your idea for a million-dollar app your casual screw can later blackmail you about."

"This isn't exactly blackmail," she pointed out. "This girl just wants to ruin him, no compensation necessary."

Across the table, Carter flipped through the papers Jade had passed to him, frown lines creasing his brow.

"This is blatant bull," Carter said drily. "Jaxon is a lot of things, but he's not a thief. The first app he created made millions. It's doing better than the one this girl claims to have had the idea for."

"Unfortunately, in this instance, truth doesn't matter. This girl—" Jade flipped through the file for her name "—Nessa Bannon, looks great on camera and has something to say about the so-called rich playboy who stole her idea and just plain took advantage of her. The world is practically salivating to get more of her story."

Within a matter of hours, social media had latched on to the few details Nessa Bannon tossed out there. The fires were being lit to roast Jaxon Diallo alive, and his family's reputation along with him. Not good news as far as the IPO was concerned.

"We need to shut all that down. Fast." Kingsley steepled his fingers. "Which is why we're here this afternoon—"

"Instead of in Las Vegas, enjoying the showgirls and casinos," Carter grumbled.

"Is that what we pulled you away from?" Kingsley didn't sound sorry, showing instead a brotherly lack of care about the relaxation he'd taken Carter away from.

Not that Jade cared that much either but neither one was her brother.

"That damn kid…" Carter muttered across from her. The tightness at the corners of his eyes betrayed his worry.

For what, Jade couldn't tell. The IPO? The scorned woman lashing out at a man she thought betrayed her? His lost all-you-can-eat Vegas buffet?

"I'm sure you've had your share of romantic road-kill from back in your younger days." She arched an eyebrow at him. Jade didn't have any proof but she mentally put a point on her side of the game when Carter flinched.

But he didn't stay down for long. "You already have the details of our planned IPO offering and about Jaxon and this mess. Do you think you can help us? Be hon-

est. If it's too much, let us know and we'll find someone else."

It was like he'd thrown down a gauntlet, and the
glint in his eyes told Jade he knew exactly what he
was doing. But what he asked wasn't impossible. Of
course, she could help them.

The situation had the potential to be an easy fix but
she could also see why Carter had lobbed this potential bomb into her lap. The last thing the Diallo family wanted to do was seem like they were covering for
an opportunist who stole from a girl trying to do better for herself.

Nessa Bannon was raised poor, was now working
to pay her own way through college, and had an Instagram account filled with gorgeous selfies and intimate details of her everyday life, including her desire
to get into fashion one day. Obviously, a beautiful and
driven girl.

Jaxon, at barely nineteen years old, was a proven
genius and already one of the leading minds in tech.
A young and very attractive member of the superrich
Diallo family of Miami, he had every advantage growing up. Good schools, resources, people paving the
way for his success.

Which of these nineteen-year-olds was more likely
to have come up with the idea for the million-dollar
app in question? The answer was clear.

But news bites were everything. The right set of
headlines read by the right people could crush the Diallos' dreams of taking their company public at a profit.

Jade wouldn't let that happen, though.

She closed the manila in front of her. "Yes, I can take care of this."

Kingsley leaned back with a relieved smile. "That's usually Carter's line. But I'm glad you have the same amount of confidence as my brother." He flicked a smile Carter's way.

Oh really? Jade flashed both of them her teeth. "More," she said. "I have much more confidence than Carter. After all, you guys came to me, right?"

"Lord, not another one!" Kingsley rolled his eyes but he was smiling. "At least when you two get this thing sorted out, I can save myself the trouble and just thank you both at the same time."

What? "Both?"

"Yes. It's your call how you handle this but I need you to work closely with Carter on it. He knows what the company is doing. And he knows the family. He'll be your shadow while you handle this."

Just great. She clenched her teeth but managed a smile. "Sounds good."

"Perfect!" Kingsley glanced at his watch then clapped his hands once. "Now, I need my office back. I have a very important lunch date in about five minutes."

Just then, the intercom buzzed on his desk phone. "Ms. Palmer-Mitchell is here to see you, Mr. Diallo."

"Ah, she's early." His face lit up like the sun.

If this was a business meeting, Jade would eat her blue Manolo Blahniks. She lazily swung her foot, wearing said shoe, and watched the door to see who would come in.

"Send her right in, Charmaine." Like a kid expecting Santa Claus, Kingsley hopped up from the conference table and opened the door in time for a slender woman with wide eyes and amazing skin to walk through it. She carried a picnic basket.

"Am I early?" she asked.

"No. You are exactly on time." Kingsley pressed a kiss to her cheek, just within breathing distance of her lush mouth, and although it should have been chaste and sweet, the passion between the two of them practically scorched Jade where she stood.

Okay then. Time to make her own exit.

"I'll leave you two to your *lunch meeting*," Carter said with fond laughter in his voice while Jade held herself back from making any sort of comment. After all, she'd just met Kingsley.

"I'll be in touch," she said, briefcase in hand, and headed for the open door. She deftly avoided shaking Carter's hand again, walking the long way around the conference table just so she wouldn't have to.

She knew she'd made a mistake when she saw Carter move up behind her. With every breath, she was aware of him following her.

For such a big man, his footsteps were light, nearly silent. Her shoulders prickled and smoky desire woke in her belly, twining its way between her legs then up through her breasts, her throat, her very fingertips. Jade quivered from the familiar longing.

Dammit. And she'd only been in the same room with him for an hour. She needed to get out of this building. Fast.

"Before you leave, let's have a quick talk in my of-

fice," he rumbled in his deep voice and she could practically feel his breath at the back of her neck.

Do we have to? She shoved down that whiny part of
herself and clasped both hands tight around the handle of the briefcase. If this were any other man, Jade
would tell him where to shove his offer of a conversation. But this wasn't any man, this was Carter, and he
was now a client.

"Lead the way."

Outside the door, she paused for him to walk ahead
of her.

"My office is just down there to the left," he said,
voice bland. "My name is on the door."

Jade almost rolled her eyes. Of course it was.

He stepped ahead of her and she followed him, trying her best to keep her eyes at shoulder level, or at
least on his back. But with her eyes on his back she saw
clearly just how well he had filled out since college.
His shoulders were so very broad, and his hips narrow.

Although she had never fooled herself into thinking she was over him the minute he walked out the
door and left her ten years ago, she didn't realize his
presence would affect her so strongly, or so soon. Her
body's traitorous response triggered a hot flush of fury.

Ahead of her, he opened a door identical to the one
that guarded Kingsley's office. His assistant, a capable woman with purple hair and multiple piercings,
greeted him with words Jade didn't pay much attention to. After a few moments of conversation, he left
his assistant behind and guided Jade deeper into the
space that was obviously all his.

He closed the door behind them. For all of its magnificent view of Miami, the glittering water of Biscayne Bay, the amazing blue skyline littered with white puffy clouds, the office was very plain. He obviously didn't spend much time there.

A spotless and bare mahogany desk sat in front of the floor-to-ceiling windows. The leather chair in front of it seemed comfortable and brand-new. The long conference table identical to Kingsley's looked unused. And that was all.

Jade spent a few precious seconds wondering where he spent his time before common sense came back to her. Then she let her anger handle the rest.

With the door closed between them and the rest of the world, she stopped being polite.

"What do you want, Carter?"

At first he didn't say anything. He just leaned back against his desk and watched her. His look was intent and hawkish, like he was just eating her up with his eyes. It was unnerving, and unexpected. Only years of doing business with some of the most frightening people in the world stopped Jade from squirming.

"It's good to see you again, Jade," he said in his basement-deep voice.

I will not react, she told herself. *I will not react.*

But it was useless. Back in college, she'd always been surprised by the low voice coming from such a skinny guy. The depth of his voice definitely matched his personality. Even then, he had been stable, reliable and so sure of himself. He handled every situation that came at him with a maturity surprising for someone that young.

At least that was what Jade realized now.

Most twenty-year-old guys didn't possess the maturity to get other college students to calm down and keep the situation peaceful. They didn't know how to effortlessly get girls to trust them and *not* take advantage of that trust by taking them to bed.

It's good to see you again, Jade, Carter had said. Did he really think so?

"I don't see anything good about this, Carter."

At least she didn't want to. Ten years should've been long enough for her to forget about what happened between them and move on. But apparently, she was as stuck in the past as her parents had been.

"I came back to Berkeley and you were gone," he said, immediately facing the elephant between them.

"Funny. I dropped by your room *the day after* we had sex and you were gone." She tipped an eyebrow at him. "A little difference there." If he wanted to talk, then dammit, they would talk. She took a seat in the sofa and put her briefcase next to her. "When did you come back to campus? A few days later? A week?" She knew the answer was neither because, fool that she had been, she waited even longer to hear from him.

He shifted against the desk, recrossing his arms. "About two weeks," he admitted after a round of jaw flexing.

"Yeah…" She pursed her lips and found to her annoyance that his eyes latched instantly to them. He was such a *man*. "Did you expect me to sit there and wait for you to decide…whatever?"

"I didn't think you'd just disappear from school, just like that," Carter said, a touch of…something in his voice. "And then I couldn't find you."

Just how well did you look? But she wasn't getting into that game with him. After he disappeared, she'd taken it stupidly hard, running back to her parents and seeking a shelter with them that she'd absolutely not found. It hadn't been a game of hide and come seek. She'd been deadly serious and thought she'd left everything to do with Carter far behind her. Except for that one important thing.

And now he was here. They were here together, dancing around something that was dead and should've been long buried.

Jade needed it to be in the ground. Maybe then, it wouldn't hurt so much.

"There was no reason to find me, Carter. That afternoon, I was stupid. I was just shocked I read Hudson wrong, that's all. I didn't know he and I were in an open relationship. Believe me, after I walked in on him and my replacement, I knew."

Jade hadn't always had a boyfriend in college. She'd gotten there single and naive and fallen immediately in love with Carter. But after nearly two years of pining after him, she agreed to be Hudson's girlfriend.

Worst. Decision. Ever.

That disaster lasted until their senior year when Hudson cheated on her, using the excuse that Jade never put out so he'd *needed* to get his sex fix from somewhere else.

"You knew, huh? What exactly did you know?" Carter adjusted his stance against the desk. A tall mountain of a man with blazing brown eyes. Watching her.

"I knew I was better off with my boyfriend. Yeah,

he was with another girl, but I was just angry. I was jealous. I wanted to get back at him and show him I could have some fun somewhere else too."

"Somewhere else?" His look sharpened.

God, she wished she knew what he was thinking. But that transparent boy had vanished out of her life ten years ago never to be seen again.

"Yes. Somewhere else. I'm sorry I made it seem like more than what it was. I just wanted to see how different it could be with another guy. You were protective and it felt good to touch somebody who was..." Tender. Always good to me. "...just different in bed."

Part of that was true, at least. Carter had been tender with her that afternoon in his sun-drenched dorm room. He'd kissed the tears from her face, licked her all over and touched every part of her that could give pleasure.

He'd been nothing like Hudson. Carter had gotten much further with his gentle touches and kisses than Hudson ever got with his threats of telling everyone how frigid she was. In the end, though, Carter had been just as bad. Worse.

That day, she'd been furious with her cheating boyfriend, and miserable. She only wanted comfort from Carter, the one person who showed her consistent kindness and understanding. But he used her body and discarded her, left her feeling worse than when she'd walked into his room.

Jade would never let him know that, though.

"I was just using you, Carter," she snapped, finally stating it bluntly since he didn't seem to get it when she used nicer words. "I just wanted a different man in bed for a change. Don't think if you'd come back any sooner there could've been anything between us."

Anticipating an angry reaction, maybe even something physical, Jade clenched her teeth and braced herself, hands curling around the edge of the couch.

But Carter only gave her that same devouring stare. His expression gave nothing away.

What the hell was she even doing?

This was stupid, trying to get a rise out of him. And why?

Jade sighed and trailed fingers through her low-cut hair. "Anyway, it doesn't matter. All that is in the past and we're working together now so that's that."

"What if I don't want that to be it?"

"I don't care what you want," Jade said.

Growling low in his throat, he pushed himself off the desk and moved toward her, but before he could reach where she sat, Jade jumped up from the sofa and grabbed her briefcase. Finally, a reaction out of him. But maybe not something she was ready for.

Carter slid himself between her and the door, a halfway-there obstacle to her freedom. "Wait," he said.

"No. I did that when I was a dumb kid but that's not my style anymore."

His Adam's apple slid up and down as he swallowed. "How long did you wait for me?"

An emotion moved across his face. Hope? Whatever it was looked out of place. This placid and nearly emotionless version of him would take some getting used to. At least until it was time for her to finish up in Miami and leave again.

If the handle of her briefcase were a neck, she

would've strangled it by now. Why were they even talking about this? Yes, she was still mad, but it was nothing a strong glass of whiskey and another ten years couldn't cure.

Jade released a slow breath. "You know what? It doesn't matter."

Suddenly feeling hollowed out, she twisted away from his infuriatingly calm face and headed for the door. She couldn't look at him another second.

"Where are you going?" he called after her. "We still have to talk." Carter hesitated. "About your work with the Diallo Corporation."

"*We* don't have anything else to talk about. Your troublemaking brother and I, though, he and I need to have a conversation sometime soon. Preferably in the next one to two days." She gripped the door handle and wrenched it open. "Now, if you have nothing else to say, I'm going to go earn the ridiculous amount of money your company is paying mine."

Without looking back, she walked out. The secretary didn't look up from her computer when Jade walked past, the height of professionalism. How many pissed-off women had she seen walking out of Carter's office over the years?

Not that it mattered to her. None of it did.

She just had to do this job then get the hell out of Miami and back to San Diego where she belonged.

Carter Diallo was a heartbreaker. He'd pummeled hers to bits before and she didn't have a spare to offer him for a repeat performance. No matter how good he looked in a suit.

Chapter 3

Someone once told Jade she wasn't the forgiving type.

It wasn't true. She forgave plenty.

She just never forgot or gave people the chance to screw her over again.

Jade didn't want to be that person, but she could only be who her parents raised her to be.

With her head swimming from their conversation, she left Carter's office. Her exact destination was unclear as hell, but who needed a destination when getting out of his presence had been the only priority?

In the Diallo Corporation parking lot, she climbed into the silver Aston Martin Vanquish she'd had shipped ahead from San Diego so she could drive it while in Miami. It was an expense. Too much, really. But her parents had raised her to be cheap and thrifty and now, these days, she wanted to throw all of that away. So the Aston Martin it was.

Sleek, seductive and sexy. Basically, the car was everything she wished she was.

And it was what she'd felt like in Carter's arms the one time they'd been in bed together. Despite the tears and her anger at Hudson, that afternoon with Carter had been a revelation. For once, she'd allowed herself to…just be. No fears, no expectations, simply pleasure and a heart-opening recklessness.

She'd never felt that way with anyone again.

Jade breathed in a deep lungful of the Miami autumn air and started the car. The Vanquish came to life with a sensual growl she could never get enough of.

"Hey!"

She nearly jumped out of her skin when she saw a girl standing next to the car. The girl had appeared there like a ghost. Skinny and big-eyed, waiting there in cutoff shorts and an electric-blue tube top that showed off more slender limbs, daggers masquerading as collarbones, a fierce look in her wide brown eyes.

"Can I get a ride?"

"What?" Jade didn't know this girl from Eve, and there was no way she was going to let a scrawny stranger into her car. She could be a crackhead for all Jade knew.

"No. Not from me," Jade said with a shake of her head.

"Hey, whatever happened to the kindness of strangers?"

If she didn't know better, she could swear the girl was making fun of her.

"This is the big city, stranger. And this is the year two thousand and whatever." Jade waved off the actual year as unimportant. "No one is *kind* for free."

"So what are you gonna charge me? I need a ride."

You have to be kidding me. This girl had to be crazy.

Or maybe you're the crazy one, still parked and talking to this girl when you could've easily pulled off and left her in a cloud of dust.

The voice inside her head could be a bitch sometimes.

But she was still vibrating from the conversation with Carter. Willing herself to think about business, and nothing else. Certainly not about the way his dark and spicy cologne had smelled good enough to lick. And the way it made her remember…everything.

Jade didn't want to face herself yet. And that self was the only thing waiting for her back in her hotel room, or even back with her parents' lawyer.

Jade reached over and opened the passenger-side door. "Where do you want to go?"

The girl threw her a grin and slid into the car, long bare legs flashing in her high-waisted denim shorts, red Converse sneakers the same bright shade as her lipstick.

"Wherever you're heading is good," the girl said. She looked around the car and gave an impressed whistle. "This is a sweet ride."

"I thought you said you need a ride somewhere."

"I do. Just out of here. Where you're going is good. As long as I don't have to be here."

Jade should've kicked her out of the car then. But the careless way the way the girl spoke, like she didn't really care where they went and just wanted an escape, spoke to exactly what she was feeling.

She put the car in gear and took off.

The girl giggled and threw her head back in the seat. "This is some monster you got. I bet you get in trouble speeding all the time."

I wish. The truth is nothing so interesting.

"Not really. I brought it with me here from San Diego but I probably won't drive it much."

"What do you mean? Miami is Flashy-car Town, USA. We probably passed a couple of million-dollar rides pulling out of the building."

The building's parking garage hadn't been all that impressive when Jade arrived. All she'd wanted to do aside from make sure no one hit her baby, was to get into the building and get the job done. Now she was too keyed up to notice more than this random girl begging a ride.

"You know you shouldn't jump in strangers' cars like this. You never now where they'll take you."

"I can take care of myself," the girl said, settling more comfortably into the black leather seat. She pulled a pair of sunglasses from on top of her head and slid them over her eyes. "The last thing you'd ever have to worry about is me," she said with a quick sideways grin.

Something about that smile and arrogant tilt of her nose struck Jade as familiar, but she couldn't put her finger on it.

"Where are we going, anyway?" the girl asked.

Really, what the hell was she doing hitching a ride in the parking lot of Diallo Corporation? Had she just wandered off the main road and decided to check it out? There were definitely more interesting places out there. This was Miami after all.

Jade flicked on her turn signal and changed lanes

close to a slow-moving black Mercedes. "I'm driving to a place up north, near Boca Raton."

The declaration jumped from her lips, unsummoned.
Okay. I guess we're going to my parents' house.

She'd told Carter she needed to work on his PR crisis but truthfully, she needed to get up to her parents' house and take a look at it. She'd been putting it off for far too long. Three days in Miami and all she'd seen were the inside of the lawyer's office, her hotel room and the car.

Looking at the house and deciding what to do with her parents' things was *the* reason she was here. Being a coward usually wasn't her way. But she was breaking a lot of new ground this week.

She cringed, remembering how she'd practically run out of Carter's office with her tail between her legs.

"Boca..." The girl leaned over to mess with the dual temperature control. Cool air gushed from the vents on her side. "Where the old folks are, huh? Thinking of buying a place up there?"

God, that sounded like a nightmare.

"No, not really," Jade muttered, barely resisting a shudder of distaste.

"Good." The girl fiddled with the radio, scrolled through a few stations before plucking her phone from her back pocket and pairing it with the car's Bluetooth. "If I ever bought a place, I'd stick to Miami. It's pretty boring up there."

If she ever bought a place... Jade eyed the girl. Nothing about her stuck out as particularly poor. The little cloth fanny pack around her waist looked like any you could pick up for a couple of dollars at the fair, her Chucks were clean and seemed relatively new, and the rest of her was clean too. She smelled like fresh oranges.

"My parents lived up there," Jade finally said after giving up on guessing what was up with the girl.

"That sounds about right. What, they realized they'd die of boredom if they stayed up there?"

"No, they just died."

She felt the girl's eyes on her, like she was checking to see if Jade was lying. "That's rough," she finally said. "Sorry."

Jade was still trying to figure out if *she* was sorry. "It's fine. We weren't close."

"Seriously? I can't imagine not being close to my family. Even when they're being asses."

"That's good. It means you love them."

"Yeah, I do..." She turned a brilliant smile to Jade then leaned back in her seat, tapping her feet to the music, sexy and hard-driving reggaeton Jade had never heard in her life. The woman on the track rapped about a man who'd done her wrong on the dance floor. And she planned on doing the same to him. Repeatedly. The song sounded good though, so she didn't complain.

The girl chattered on about the specs of the car, obviously excited. All these things Jade knew about it; after all, those were the reasons she bought the car in the first place. "And it must be custom. I've never seen one like this at the car shows." She touched the buttons and the gleaming surfaces, clearly appreciative, but not at all covetous. It was interesting to watch. Refreshing.

Then she took a series of selfies with the car's controls in the background.

"So," the girl said when she'd finished her photo shoot. Her impish smile showed itself again along with the ultrasharp-looking canines that made her look both wild and oddly childlike. "My name is Dee, what's yours?"

Names. Right. Asking the young stranger's name probably would've been the sensible thing to do before she even got into the car.

Jade tilted a look at the girl but kept an eye on the road. Dee, huh?

She was tempted to tell her *J* and see what the girl would make of it, getting a fake name in exchange for a fake name. Whatever her name was, that was a crap attempt at subterfuge. Why, though? It wasn't like Jade was interested enough in the girl to try to find out her real name. No reason at all to do that. Although young, she seemed over eighteen. If she had parents that she had run away from, the girl had her reasons. Although from what she'd said earlier, her family meant the world to her.

"My name's Jade."

The girl cracked a laugh. "Was your mom a fan of China or something?"

Jade shrugged. "No. That was the name my father's favorite girlfriend went by." Probably wasn't even her real name.

Dee stared at her, wide-eyed. "For real?"

Jade shrugged again. It was one of those things she'd grown up knowing, something her mother had thrown at her father during one of their arguments that Jade never forgot. She didn't even know if they'd been aware she was there, twelve years old and shocked.

Not just that her parents were having an argument—one of the two she remembered—but that her mother had allowed it. Hearing that revelation, she realized then at twelve why her mother very rarely called her by her name. It was "honey" or "sweetie" or something along those lines. Only when her mother was mad did she become "Jade."

"It's just life," she said to Dee. "Some facts are pretty, some aren't."

"God… I'm sticking my foot real deep in it every five seconds with you." Dee slumped back in the seat, the corners of her lips drooping down. She stopped tapping her feet to the music. "Damn."

Jade's mouth twitched and she clenched her hand on the gearshift to stop herself from patting the girl in reassurance. It was her tragedy after all, not Dee's.

The silence from anything but the music felt almost oppressive and Jade bit her lip to stop herself from filling it with her own pointless rambling. This was what waited for her in her hotel room. This and the trying to forget.

But was going to her parents' house any better?

The side street to her hotel was coming up fast. She eyed it, then watched it pass by. The car rumbled as she shifted and passed a pair of white Priuses in a blur. She needed to get off the major streets. The fastest way to get a cop on her butt was to speed around here. She raced toward the highway, up the on-ramp and darted into the car pool lane, flying fast.

"Cool! This car can really take off!" Dee giggled, her good mood returning with the car's speed.

Who the hell was this girl?

Hell, who was Jade in this moment?

This woman who ran from her problems wasn't the real her. Ever since her parents left her to fend for herself, she'd faced everything head-on, convinced that nothing but more pain lay the way of postponing the inevitable.

So far, the only thing she'd been wrong about was the direction of the pain. It wasn't a single arrow shooting into you once your feet turned in the wrong direction. Instead, it was an ocean, spreading out on all sides, deep and overwhelming. This pain was one of life's certainties.

"It's one of the reasons I got it," Jade said with a twist of her lips. "I thought it would help me run away from my problems."

Dee chortled. "You're over twenty-five so you must know better by now."

Jade looked the slight girl up and down. "Are *you* over twenty-five?"

The girl rolled her eyes. "Obviously you're making a joke. I'm just mature for my age." She took another selfie, this one with duck lips, her bright red mouth pointed at the camera like a weapon.

All too soon, they got to the house Jade had been avoiding for days.

"This place is nice." Dee stepped out of the car and onto the driveway.

Jade firmly closed the driver's side door, staring up at the two-story colonial-style house she grew up in. "Yeah, it is."

As a kid, she hadn't thought they had that much money. Enough to keep her in the latest random stuff she wanted, finance a vacation for the three of them someplace in the Caribbean twice a year and pay the mortgage on the house.

Through the eyes of an adult, she saw that they had been solidly upper middle class, her father a family lawyer and her mother an accountant who mostly worked from home. From what the lawyer's documents said, the house, three blocks from the lake in a respectable Hollywood neighborhood, was now worth a little over eight hundred thousand dollars. Or a million, if you rounded up.

Jade took the keys out of her pocket and began the walk up the long driveway.

"Why are we here anyway? It looks deserted." Dee shoved her phone in the back pocket of her tiny shorts and hiked toward the front door at Jade's side.

At nearly five o'clock in the afternoon, the house did look deserted. No cars in the driveway but Jade's. Sensor lights clicking on above the door although it wasn't dark enough for them do any work. The lawn was neatly cut. Immaculate. But the yard and house felt completely empty. And they hadn't even gotten inside yet.

"I'm here because I need to sell it," Jade said with a wry twist of her lips. Already, she could feel a tide of something unpleasant pushing at her from her house. Sadness, most likely. Memories. "I'm not sure why *you're* here."

Which was a bit of a lie. She was there as Jade's distraction. Or a messed-up idea of moral support. Depending on how truthful she was being with herself at the moment.

"Don't be mean," Dee said with a tiny frown. She

took a quick picture of the house then shoved her phone back into her pocket.

With a twist of the key, Jade unlocked the door. Immediately, the alarm began to wail.

Her parents always had the alarm on, even when they were home. It always made Jade feel trapped. Even leaving her room to get a glass of juice in the middle of the night filled her with dread.

Damn motion sensors. Damn her parents.

Her father had been a controlling hypocrite and the worst of liars. He had a mistress, always quoted the Bible, forbade Jade from knowing anything about birth control and made sure she went to college as innocent as a lamb being led to slaughter. And her mother had let it all happen.

Heart pounding, Jade put in the code the lawyer had given her to silence the screaming alarm and stepped into the house she hadn't been inside for years. She flicked on the light switch in the hallway.

"Wow…"

Yeah. *Wow* was right.

The inside of the house looked nothing like the old and antiquated place she remembered. Reddish hardwoods, maybe bamboo, gleamed in the entranceway. A pretty, modern chandelier glittered above their heads. And, as they walked down the hallway and through the rooms, Jade saw that the furniture was all very current, very vibrant.

The house felt so empty. Like they'd renovated it just before they died and never got to enjoy it before the car crash stole their lives.

Staring at everything she saw, Dee went one way

in the house and Jade went another. It was as beautiful throughout as it was at the entryway. Elegant, updated, contemporary. What had once been a massive living room had been transformed into a large bedroom suite—bedroom, sitting room, giant walk-in closet—looking out over the pool. The king-size bed was made up with what looked and smelled like brand-new sheets. Even the very air of the room, of the whole house, smelled crisp and untouched. Like Dee said, deserted.

In the kitchen, Jade found stainless steel appliances, a ceramic cooktop and harlequin-tiled floors. Nothing of the dark and kitschy setup she remembered.

This was a home for a modern couple. Which her parents had definitely *not* been.

"Oh my God!" Dee's voice came from upstairs.

Jade ran up there to see what Dee was freaking out about. In the hallway, she froze. Or at least what had once been the hallway leading to the other three bedrooms upstairs. All that had been gutted and renovated and turned into...nothing.

"This is amazing!" Dee twirled in the center of the large space.

It was all one big room with a bathroom on each end, tall and gleaming columns of wood breaking up the monotony of the oversize room, like they had been load bearing and couldn't be removed.

The wall and doors that had once stood between the upstairs patio and two of the bedrooms was now a screen of sliding glass doors looking down to the pool, the rest of the pristine backyard, a garden and the lake.

Nothing was like Jade remembered. Her parents had basically torn out every trace of what the house was.

Dark. Oppressive. And old, but *not* in a cool way.

Now it felt like a completely different house.

Jade didn't realize she'd been spinning in disoriented circles, trying to take it all in until she stumbled into one of the columns. She slammed into the textured wood hard enough to bruise. She gasped on a breath of pain.

"Are you okay?" Dee appeared at her side.

"Yeah, yeah."

Nothing here was what she had expected. Yes, she'd felt the roll of familiar anxiety when she stood outside the door, but all that was gone now. She might as well have been standing in a stranger's home.

In some ways, maybe that was what it was.

Jade took a breath, then swept her gaze around the entire top floor. Yes, she could easily sell this. With the way the real estate market was right now, if she listed the house at even a decent asking price, it would probably get an offer in less than a week. Then it would be out of her life for good. Just like her parents.

She took another breath. "You ready?"

Dee looked confused. "Sure. But that's it? That's all you wanted to do? Literally just look around?"

"Of course. And now I'm finished." She rattled the keys in her hand. "Let's go."

For a moment, Dee looked like she was going to ask more questions, but she just huffed and stomped down the stairs while Jade followed her on more silent feet.

This was the house her parents left behind. Now gutted and rearranged and looking like something Jade had never seen before.

This was all that was left of them. This was all that

was left of the life she'd lived with them. Just a giant empty space. She swallowed hard.

A sharp pain spasmed under her breastbone and Jade rubbed over the spot. No, she was not sad. It was all just finally over.

She got into the car and started the powerful engine while Dee huffed some more in the passenger seat. "That was so lame," the girl said.

"Probably. I didn't promise you any excitement on this outing."

I don't even recall inviting you along, Jade thought but kept that last bit to herself.

"So true." Dee buckled herself in. "Fine." Her phone beeped and she reached into her back pocket for it. Staring at the phone, she made a happy noise. Her eyes gleamed when she looked up at Jade. "You wanna go someplace I want now?"

What was the alternative? Head back to the hotel and work? Drive herself crazy wondering why her parents gutted the house they loved so much? Try not to think about Carter and all the ways he effortlessly destroyed her peace of mind?

Jade shrugged and gave Dee her most carefree smile. "Sure."

Chapter 4

Jade was seriously pissed at Carter.

After trying to convince him she'd used him in college, she'd stormed out and left him shocked in her wake. Shocked not because she'd used him as a sex toy that one glorious afternoon in September, but shocked that she'd even attempt the lie.

He may not have been very experienced in college, but even a guy as oblivious as him knew a virgin when he slept with one. On his dorm bed with the two of them naked and face-to-face, she'd been trembling and nervous. When he touched her, she blushed. She'd been amazed at his body, the way it hardened for her and sought eagerly to plunge into her delicate, feminine flesh.

Then there was the blood.

All these years after, he still vividly remembered the

details of that bright afternoon. Her wide eyes when she saw him naked. The trembling tips of her breasts under his tongue. Her soft, kittenish cries as he kissed between her thighs.

Jade had been so tight, he'd barely been able to get inside her. Still shivering in the wake of the orgasms he'd given her with his tongue and fingers, she whimpered from that first stroke. Then she couldn't get enough of him.

The memory of that afternoon seeped into Carter like a drug.

Chill. You're at work.

He stood in the middle of his office, staring at the closed door she'd disappeared through less than ten minutes before.

Jade Tremaine.

The woman who'd driven him crazy with lust and protectiveness in college.

The woman who still haunted his dreams.

The initial buzz of shock from her presence had worn off during the meeting with her and Kingsley. The whole time, Carter hadn't been able to stop staring at her. She was even more beautiful than before. The hair she used to wear long and straight in college was now cut short and natural. That wild, sensual energy she had back then, all a teasing possibility in her lean and curvaceous frame, had grown to its full potential. More than even before, she looked like an angel. A sensual, unforgiving one. But an angel just the same.

The office phone chimed suddenly, pulling him from his obsessive thoughts about Jade.

"Yes, Caroline?"

"Your sister called," his assistant said over the intercom. "She wants you to meet her at Liquid Crush."

Was it that time again? A sigh gusted from Carter's lips.

Apparently, Paxton had made it her mission of the year to get him to relax. At first, she invited him to different parties and functions all over Miami. Sending texts to let him know a ticket waited for him at the door. Sometimes it was just a note about his favorite artists being in town. Most of the time, he didn't go. He had a lot on his plate.

Between keeping the more irresponsible members of his family from ending up in jail or worse, making sure the company was safe in more ways than one and trying various methods to get Jade out of his subconscious, he was a busy guy.

Paxton didn't want to hear any of it. So she'd stopped sending the messages to his phone and instead sent them directly to his assistant, making the events seem like appointments. Caroline knew damn well what Paxton was doing. But she apparently thought he needed to relax too. Meddling women.

One of the youngest of them and one of the last set of twins, Paxton was a typical Diallo. But where her siblings were driven and very controlling, she was a genius and just a little bit crazy. A lot like her twin, Jaxon. Who was officially the reason Jade Tremaine was back in Carter's life.

Carter wanted to wring Jaxon's neck a little. But he also wanted to hug the kid.

"Caroline, you know I can't do that. I have another meeting." Technically, that wasn't true.

"Technically, that's not true." Caroline parroted his thoughts in a creepy way he'd come to accept over the years.

Sighing, Carter dropped his head back in the chair

Yes, what he had was an appointment for a massage. One that Caroline had quickly put together for him since he had to come back to work so early after Vegas instead of taking the little break he'd planned.

"But if you insist on calling it that, fine," she continued. "Your *meeting* is in an hour in Morningside. Paxton has your tickets to Liquid Crush waiting for you at the door. There's no time you have to be there but she suggested you get there in about two hours. Maybe three if you're feeling too relaxed to move."

Why did he ever think it was a good idea to get an assistant? He was the fixer of the family. He could control his own damn schedule.

"As always, it's your call," Caroline said, playing her best card. "But you know she wants you to be there. She says she never sees you anymore."

Damn both these women. But Carter shook his head, fighting a smile.

"Okay. Let me just get myself together and head out to the masseuse. I'll see how I feel after." But they both knew he would go and meet his sister.

After a long and luxurious massage that left him feeling boneless and ready to confess his worst sins to the massage therapist, Carter went home to change, grabbed a quick ten-minute nap to power up then left his house for the club.

He wasn't sure what Paxton had in mind.

She knew he wasn't the reggaeton-and-rum type. He

also wasn't into electronic music or the meat market they called *clubs* either. When he picked up women, it was in one of his natural habitats. The airport. His gym. Once he'd even met a woman at the car dealership where he'd gotten his Bugatti.

The clubs just weren't his scene. The few times he did go, it was to places that catered to picky bastards like him.

Which was apparently just what Paxton had found.

He walked into Liquid Crush, and immediately felt relaxed. The woman at the door—a model-gorgeous specimen in a tight tuxedo jacket, leather pants and high heels—immediately knew who he was.

"Follow me, Mr. Diallo," she said after giving him a warm but impersonal smile. A definite signal she wasn't there for *his* entertainment.

She held a flashlight between her slender fingers, and after exchanging a more genuine smile with the hostess, guided Carter through the crowded—but not *over*crowded—club.

In the high heels, she was nearly as tall as he was and it was either that or her sheer confidence that kept her moving steadily through the club with not a single *excuse me*. He kept pace behind her and didn't miss the lustful glances most of the men they passed threw her way.

The place glittered like the set of a TV spaceship. Cool blue lights. Innovative seating. A DJ playing music he loved—'90s music with occasional Top 40 hits. The mood was chill.

A pair of women brushed past him. Bare shoulders. Thick bodies. One of them turned to him as she passed and looked over her shoulder at him, all lush lips and sweet invitation.

Him? He barely stopped himself from looking down at himself to see what she was looking at in such an interested way. But one thing he'd learned about women over the years was that they were too mysterious for him to figure out.

When he was out with his brothers, most of them six-and-a-half feet tall and movie-star handsome, the women who tended to pick them like oranges from a backyard tree habitually chose him last, if at all. Most of the women Carter ended up in bed with had gotten there because of his skillful and steady pursuit. Most women didn't want muscle in a suit. Unless, like the woman on the plane, they wanted what the suit itself symbolized.

Wealth. Money. VIP Passes.

Carter knew he was too big, too plain looking—at least in comparison to his brothers—for most. And practically every day, he was just fine with that.

"Here you are, Mr. Diallo?"

The place the hostess took him to was obviously VIP. It was elevated above the rest of the bar by a short flight of stairs, a level that held five other VIP booths sheltered from each other by frosted glass walls.

The VIP area was perfectly placed. High enough to have a view of and access to the dance floor, but distant enough that he could keep himself away from most of the other clubgoers or have a private conversation—or semipublic sex—if he wanted to.

"Thank you," he said.

"It's our pleasure."

The leather seats were plush and warm—no cooling leather to get used to—and soft enough that he immediately felt comfortable. They instantly invited him to sink in and let any worries float away. The woman straightened with another of her warm smiles just as a server appeared behind her, a man in the same outfit, this time with a tray holding a pair of whiskey glasses, a bucket of ice and a small platter of calamari.

"With our compliments," the woman said. "If you need anything, Paulo will be checking on you throughout the evening."

Carter thanked her again and after a few exchanged words with Paulo, she was gone.

The place was big, but not too big, and the music was just right. Somehow, maybe through noise dampeners, the music wasn't as loud up in the VIP area as on the dance floor. He could actually hear himself think.

The club and VIP were very nice. He could easily fool himself into thinking this place was private, made just for him with the sensuous bodies moving on the dance floor, the music and the bottle of his favorite whiskey in front of him.

But he tried not to fool himself very often.

"Carter! You came!"

He looked up in time to see Paxton dancing her way toward him. His sister's smile was brilliant. With a clear drink in hand, she looked happy about how her evening was going. Carter smiled back at her then laughed when she flopped down in the seat next to him, bouncing in the soft leather. Amazingly, she didn't spill a single drop of her drink.

She looked good. Not at all like the sulky recent

high school grad he saw a few days ago when they'd talked about Jaxon and all the crap he was getting into lately. Her face was more relaxed and, in her shorts and skimpy blouse, she looked ready for a casual Saturday at the neighborhood pool.

"What are you wearing?"

She giggled and flopped her sneakered feet up on the table in front of the leather couch. "Clothes, obviously."

The massage had worked well on him. His body was loose and his muscles felt smoothed and softened. If all he had to do was go home and climb into his bed tonight, he'd be very happy. Which must have been why he didn't growl at her about being a smart-ass.

"God! I can't believe you actually came." She grinned around the straw stuck in her drink. "I was about to give up on you."

"Feel free to give up. I'm a figment of your imagination. Just like you're a figment of mine," he said. "I could swear this is a twenty-five-and-up bar."

She giggled again and poked him in the side. "Don't worry about that, grandpa. I won't do anything crazy like let them see me drinking here." Paxton shook her glass at him. "This is just soda water."

Like most of the family, she was hyperaware of their image now that the company was ready to go public. Generally, she did what she wanted. But she was also the more responsible of the twins. She'd never do anything to deliberately hurt the family or their business. She and Carter had talked about that enough times in the past. Too much for a kid her age, he thought.

She was vibrant and wild, young enough to want

her pleasure on tap. He wanted that for her. Not the mountain of responsibility he'd eagerly grabbed on to at her age.

"What are you doing here, anyway?" he asked her.

"I brought a friend. She needed to relax. We were just about to leave when I got the text that you were here." She bumped him with her shoulder. "Nice one. Way to keep us guessing. I texted Leo and told him. He doesn't believe you actually showed up."

"I'm sure our brother has better things to do than worry about my social life."

"He actually doesn't." She looked serious for a moment, then cracked another smile. "I'm heading back to the dance floor. Don't be surprised if Leo shows up." She smacked an orange-scented kiss on his cheek then was off again.

She had too much damn energy…

Smiling, he poured himself a double shot of whiskey and prepared to sit back and enjoy the drink. He'd give the club another hour before heading back home.

"Oh!" Paxton popped up again. "They're about to play your song. Come dance with me."

She didn't take no for an answer, and he didn't even bother to give it. A quick sip of his whiskey and then they were off. The dance floor was packed. Gorgeous women. Men who were dancing as well as the women they were trying to get into bed that night. The music was loud and the bass shuddered into his body and crept up his spine.

Tupac's "California Love" shook the place.

He *loved* this song.

Beside him, Paxton jumped and danced, looking more

like a young teenager than a recently turned nineteen-year-old. When the song ended, she briefly leaned close. "I'll be right back. Don't go anywhere." She was good at disappearing and did it again with another one of her cheerful smiles.

Coolio's "Gangsta's Paradise" started and made him smile.

A soft body bumped him from behind and stumbled. He turned, ready to catch the woman in case she fell.

"Careful, mi—"

But the words fell back to wherever they came from. He damn near swallowed his tongue. The woman dancing near him took his breath away. Her long and sensuous back moved to the rhythm of the song. There was nothing erotic about it, but the way she moved transformed everything he'd ever thought about when Coolio sang "on my knees in the night."

Her head was thrown back. Elegant throat bared in her pleasure. Her slim waist moved like a snake and invited the press of his hands.

It was Jade.

Although her back was to him, he would recognize her anywhere.

She danced near him, her body on lush display in the same suit she had on at their meeting earlier today. But she had discarded the jacket, and the dark pants that had looked respectable enough on her sensuous body now seemed erotic and unbelievably sensual under the club lights.

The curve of her hips made his mouth dry. Lust throbbed in his lap and he wanted nothing more than to pull her back against him and press his suddenly aching hardness against her bottom. It didn't help that she was dancing with her eyes closed, her arms up in the air like she was all alone on the dance floor, maybe all alone in a world of her own making.

What was she doing there?

"Jade…"

Her eyes opened and blinked at him; her long lashes fluttered. It was a motion that shouldn't have looked as decadent as it did. With her arms in the air and her body rocking to the bass-heavy music, her eyes slowly opening, it seemed as if she was waking from a long sleep.

"Carter."

Her voice was husky, and rough. It reached into his chest and lower, grabbing him hard. It wrecked him.

She glanced around like she was surprised to find herself in a club and surrounded by so many people. Or maybe she was just surprised to see him. He moved closer. There were words to say but he couldn't find them. Her body was incense and smoke and it lured him. For once, he allowed his body to rule.

He moved closer and his belly brushed hers. Electric. Had it been that way back in college? He nearly shook his head. The past was past. It had messed with him for years now. In dreams. In the regret he didn't know he'd been carrying around until he saw her in his brother's office.

That afternoon in his dorm room, she had blown his world wide-open by coming to him. Soft and needy, and then fiercely hungry, begging him to comfort her. That afternoon had been nothing like in his dreams.

But it was easy to forget with the dream riding him hard every time he closed his eyes.

It had rewritten history in him.

"Jade..."

"Carter..."

Again. Always reciprocal, the two of them. Until they weren't.

Without his permission, his arms slipped around her waist.

At first, she stiffened in his arms. "What...?" Then her lashes fell low over her eyes before flicking back up. "My parents died," she said.

The arousal stuttered and fell from him. "When?"

She swayed, moving closer, hands settling on his shoulders. He expected the smell of alcohol on her lips, but all he got was the clean scent of her breath. Her lips, nearly wiped clean of all color, lured him closer.

Jade was absolutely naked with him in that moment.

"Over a week ago." Her voice was low and her breath brushed against his lips. "A car accident."

"I'm sorry," he said.

Although he didn't know her parents and had only met them twice when they visited Jade on campus, they'd seemed nice enough. They'd been wholesome-looking church types who took Jade out to dinner once a month when they came into town and had been nice to him the times they'd briefly spoken.

"I'm not sorry," she said. The unsettled truth of it was plain on her face. "I loved them, but I'm not sure they loved me, and I'm not sure I'm sad enough that they're gone." She made a soft sound at the back of her throat. Her lashes fell low to hide her eyes. She moved closer to him. Body swaying as she danced with him, following the strains of the tune. The song was deep and a little aggressive, but her body moved to a slower, more mellow beat. Brushing against him. Teasing him.

But he willed his arousal to stay dormant. Now wasn't the time to get an erection.

"It's okay to feel something different from what the rest of the world tells you," he said. He knew all too well what he was talking about. "Not everything is as black and white as people make it seem."

"Black and white are there for a reason," she returned. "It's a guidepost for what should be."

"Really? I must have been doing things wrong then." For most of his adult life, he'd existed in shades of gray. Always doing what it took to protect his family. Nothing overtly illegal, but all that mattered, when he looked at the crisis in the moment and its possible repercussions, was his family.

Jade made a noise of denial and snuggled closer.

Ah, she felt so good.

Like ten years before, Carter wanted to protect her. He wanted to shield her from all the bad things out there in the world that would hurt someone as delicate as she was. And although she was all sharp suits and aggressive wordplay and more successful than he thought she would ever want to be, she was still Jade.

She was still Thick Brown from the girls' dorm upstairs, fresh from a sheltered life who hadn't even known what a condom was or how to use one.

With the music thumping around them, Carter made a shushing noise and tugged her closer. He rested his arms along the vulnerable line of her back and allowed her to move in the shelter of his arms. Her silk blouse brushed against his cotton shirt. Her warm breath seasoned his throat. The speakers rained down familiar music and it shoved him right back to the ball of yearning and uncertainty he had been back then.

In college, he'd only been certain of two things. His love for his family. And his ability to fix anything they needed. When Jade blew into his life, something changed, though. At the time, he had no idea what. But now...

God, she was so beautiful. Without realizing it, he'd missed this. The wanting a woman in one breath, and needing to protect her in the next.

He'd missed Jade Tremaine powerfully, and it was a miracle or some extreme denial that he was just now realizing it.

Moving together without the intrusion of conversation, he allowed her the space to simply *be* for long moments before he spoke again. "Do you want a drink?"

Her head slowly came up and she seemed to blink away whatever was at the forefront of her mind. "God, I must be more tired than I realized." Lashes flickering low over her eyes, Jade trailed long fingers down her throat and drew back. "No, I don't think that's a good idea. I..." She looked around her. "I came here with a friend, or someone I just met." She wrinkled her nose then. "I don't know where she went, though."

"She ditched you?"

"No, it's nothing like that." Jade pulled all the way back until they were no longer touching. "I should go." She dug the heel of one hand into her eye, blinked, then straightened her shoulders.

"Do you even know where you are?" Carter asked.

"No, but I have GPS on my phone." She all but rolled her eyes at him. "I'm not as helpless as I was back in college."

Internally, he winced. Of course she wasn't. For a few minutes, he may have fooled himself into thinking that a small part of the college girl still remained, but now that illusion was gone.

Jade was a grown and practical woman, fully capable of taking care of herself.

He tried to appeal to that part of her. "You look exhausted. You can sit for a minute at my table and have a coffee before you head back on the road."

Another shake of her head. "No. I think this is where I get off this ride."

"Carter!"

He looked toward the sound of his name and nearly groaned out load. His brothers Wolfe and Leo cut through the crowd toward them. Only long years of practice hiding his emotions made him nod in the direction of his brothers instead of shouting at them to get out of there and leave him alone with Jade.

They barreled toward him, their height making them easy to spot in the club. It didn't take a mind reader to see they were about to give him so much crap about Jade. Who they probably thought was just some random woman.

"What's up?" he asked when they got close enough to hear him without shouting across the club.

"The usual." Wolfe raised his voice above the music. "Pax said you were here solo and might need some adult company." Leo's grin turned mischievous. "But I guess she didn't know about your friend."

"Friend?" Jade lifted an eyebrow at Leo, then offered her hand. "I'm Jade. And you?"

"Leo, the good-looking brother." He laughed.

Wolfe shook his head and offered his own hand, introducing himself in the deep bass rumble of his voice. And Carter waited with a sick feeling in his gut for Jade to start stuttering or falling all over his brother like most women tended to.

"A pleasure," she said with a firm shake of his hand and a smile. "You look a lot like Carter."

"Yes, ma'am. I do. Not many people notice that." Wolfe's smile widened, obviously pleased when she didn't try to make a fool of herself over him. He was well aware of his looks and his effect on the general female population. Happily married for the past couple of years, and infatuated with the same woman for much longer than that, Wolfe didn't much care what other women thought of his looks. All that mattered was that his wife, Nichelle, loved him.

Unfortunately, Wolfe had to spend far too much time writing off women who had come into the picture as one of his brothers' dates and ended up trying to get him into bed.

"Ma'am? I don't recall seeing any grannies around here," Jade said. "You can just call me Jade."

"Jade, then." Wolfe grinned. "Can we buy you a drink?"

She smiled tiredly. "No, I'm good for now, thanks."

"Well, let us know if you change your mind," Wolfe said.

He gave Jade another smile before turning his attention back to Carter.

"Did Pax finally scare you into coming out or what?" Wolfe chuckled and clapped Carter on the back.

Although the crowd was intense on the dance floor, Wolfe managed to find plenty of room to move. There was something about his brother, apart from his stupid good looks, that made the rest of the world stop and sigh and take another look. The man didn't go anywhere without women falling all over him, promising him the world based on nothing but his smile and the unintentional smolder in his eyes.

Wolfe had always been that way, just as Carter had always been the plain one in their family. Once they'd all gone out together and a bitch of a girl who couldn't get Wolfe into bed called him and Carter Beauty and the Beast. It didn't take a degree in rocket science to figure out who was who in her mind.

Needless to say, she never got a chance to hit that.

"Pax didn't scare me into a damn thing," Carter muttered. "It was just time for me to get out."

"You planned on getting laid after the blackmail job, didn't you?" Leo smirked.

"That's right!" Wolfe threw his head back and laughed. "Diallo Corporation, the ultimate cock block."

Carter's brothers laughed it up real good.

He tried not to look at Jade, although he was well aware of her suddenly too-interested look at his brother's choice of conversation.

Despite not keeping his schedule on the family calendar that usually had where each sibling was working at anytime, they always seemed to know what Carter was doing. Or *not* doing.

Instead of answering, Carter not-so-playfully punched him in the arm. "I had to get back here."

Wolfe chuckled. "Come on, let me buy you a drink. We can talk better at your table."

The music had changed anyway. The dance floor wasn't as welcoming as it had been before.

Leo gestured in front of him. "Jade, join us?" His smile was wicked and charming.

The hesitation in her was obvious and Wolfe caught his eyes over Jade's head.

What's going on here? He caught his brother's question as easily as if he'd read his mind.

Carter tipped his head in an answering gesture. *I'll tell you later.*

"Sure," Jade said. "I can't stay long, though." She checked the crowd over her shoulder like she was still searching for whatever friend she had come to the club with. Then she shrugged and followed Wolfe while Leo kept pace just behind her.

The bottle of whiskey was still there but the bucket of ice was fresh and four other clean glasses sat in a group at the edge of the table. The service was ridiculously good. Wolfe dropped into the leather seat with a groan while Leo sat down next to him, deftly maneuvering Jade into sitting next to Carter.

His brothers thought they were slick.

They had only just settled in when the waiter came back. "Anything else I can get for you?"

"I'm good with this." Wolfe gestured to the whiskey, a thirty-year-old bottle he probably had a few of at home.

"Me too," Leo said.

"Just a bottle of sparkling water, please," Carter ordered while Jade just shook her head and sat back in the cushions.

"So, Jade…" Leo grinned, looking between Carter and Jade. "…what are you doing with our delightful Carter here?"

"Yes, young woman," Wolfe rumbled with an amused glint in his eye. "What are your intentions with our Carter here? You know he's a delicate guy. Don't toy with his heart if you're not going to make an honest man out of him."

Carter could've happily kicked his brother in the teeth. Both of them.

"Don't you guys have places to go?" he asked.

"Nope," Wolfe said. "We're just here for you, brother."

Leo cackled like a maniac and poured himself a glass of whiskey.

"Seriously, you guys gotta stop busting my balls." Carter grabbed the rapidly emptying whiskey bottle from Leo. "Jade is with Stoneheart Public Relations Group. She's here to deal with the fallout from the situation with Jaxon."

Wolfe whistled under his breath. "So you're the PR wizard Kingsley was talking about."

"I don't know about PR wizard, but I can make most of your PR nightmares disappear," Jade said, her tone casual and utterly confident. It was nothing more than

Carter had already heard from his business connection in New York. He said she was *magic*.

Carter was very aware of her warmth next to him in the booth. He noticed too that some of her exhaustion was falling away. Jade looked more animated, more invested in what was going on around her.

"I like her." Leo grinned. He loved anyone who didn't conform to his expectations.

When the waiter came back with the water, Carter passed it to Jade without a word. In college, she had been obsessed with sparkling water, especially La-Croix. Surprise flickered across her features as she took in the cool blue can along with a highball glass already clinking with ice.

"Thank you," she murmured. Then her eyes shuttered. She was thinking too much again.

Leo leaned close. "So what's your game plan with the Jaxon sit—"

"Nope." Carter cut Leo off. "We're not discussing business tonight. Come to one of the meetings later this week if you want in on this. Tonight is just to chill." Work life got in the way of a good time often enough. If they didn't need to discuss Jaxon and his idiocy until tomorrow or even the next day, there was no reason to bring it up now.

"Cool. All right, all right. I get it. Business later."

Coming from Leo that was pretty funny. While not as bad as Pax when it came to gutting life for the most it could give, he was as far from a workaholic as possible. He loved his life easy, simple and fun. Wolfe, who had his own company so had no dogs in the fight, nodded slowly.

"Yeah, business can always wait."

"Good, because I don't feel like trashing your brother in front of you."

On the inside, Carter winced. Cue Leo's defensiveness in three...two...one.

"But is it trashing if it's the truth, though?"

Carter stared at his brother. "Who are you and what have you done with Leonidas Diallo?"

"Leonidas?" A hint of a smile curved Jade's mouth.

"Yeah, our mother has a thing for Belgian chocolates. She saw the name when she was pregnant with Leo and his twin, Lola, and that was all she wrote."

"Yeah, she's lucky she only got stuck with Godiva for a middle name."

"Seriously?"

"Yes, my mother has been known to be very mean to her kids."

"Not on purpose, though," Leo said with a quick spread of his hands. And that alone was testament to how much he loved their mother. Carter didn't think *he* had it in him to forgive a candy-coated name.

"You're a sweetie," Jade said, with one of her heart-stopping smiles.

And Carter saw it the moment his brother realized how shockingly beautiful she was. Leo swallowed, looked at her twice then looked once at Carter who only gave him the barest lift of an eyebrow. He could practically see the moment his brother made the mental calculation, the leap, and made the decision not to take any chances. He sat back in his chair, clutching his whiskey to his chest like a teddy bear.

Good choice. Carter briefly squeezed his shoulder.

Jade looked at them both. "Did I just miss something?"

"Nope," Leo said. "Not a single thing. Um, tell me, do you have a sister?"

"What?"

Carter hid his irrepressible grin behind his drink. "Not everyone has an endless supply of siblings the way we do, Leo."

"Why not? You'd think screwing like rabbits went out of style after our parents were done."

"Maybe they just started using birth control," Wolfe said.

"How many of you are there anyway?" Jade asked.

"Thirteen," Carter said at the same time as his brothers.

Her eyebrows rose. "That's a lot of kids in one house."

"Thank you for being tactful with your response," Wolfe said drily.

A laugh tickled fiercely at the back of Carter's throat. He took another drink and swallowed it down. "Do you want a refill, Jade?" He gestured to her now empty glass and the melting ice.

"No." She exchanged a quick smile with Leo who was pouring on the charm but from a safe distance. "I should probably be going. It's late and I have to be up early tomorrow to take care of some things."

"We just got here," Leo whined.

"Not my fault you're late." Jade dropped a grin his way and Carter's brother practically preened. She stood up. "But I really have to go now. No rest for the weary and all that."

"I thought it was no rest for the wicked."

"I haven't done a single wicked thing in years," she said. "So, no. Not so much."

I doubt that, Carter thought, but didn't say anything about it. He finished the last swallow of whiskey in his glass. "Let me walk you out."

With his brothers there, she had been fun and interesting, but he had the feeling she hadn't quite been herself. Or at least hadn't felt comfortable enough to say what was on her mind.

"I'll be back," he said to his brothers and stood up, buttoning his suit jacket.

"Don't hurry back," Leo said and Wolfe tapped him firmly on the stomach; his brother made an *oof*! of sound.

Oblivious to the men's byplay, Jade had opened her mouth to say something, probably about how unnecessary it was for Carter to walk her to her car. But he moved out of the VIP booth and stepped to the side, waiting for her to join him.

"You don't have to do this, you know."

"Of course. I know all the things I have to do. This isn't one of them but I'm offering because I want to."

Jade stared at him, probably taking in how deadly serious he looked. As usual. Or as usual as she would find him now. "Okay."

"I parked my car out back in employee parking."

"Lead the way."

With his brothers behind him and Jade in front, Carter walked out to the parking lot not knowing what to expect. She wanted to say something to him. That much was obvious. But what, except maybe to "confess" to him that she'd actually been a virgin their first time together, he had no idea. They made their way through the crowded club, and outside into the cooling, still-warm-somehow Miami evening.

"This is me," she said when they stopped near a silver Aston Martin Vanquish.

God damn. The car was sleek and sexy. It was nice to see Jade standing next to it, all proprietary and so very seductive. She was a vision that made his knees go weak.

"This is a hot ride," he said.

Jade blinked in confusion, like her mind had been anyplace but this parking lot. Then her face cleared. "You have no idea," she said with a smirk. Whatever uncertain mood she had been in inside the club seemed to have disappeared completely.

Maybe her car was magic too.

Keeping her eyes on his face, she reached into her bra and took something out. It was the key fob to the car. Carter licked his lips, shamelessly watching.

"I'd love a ride sometime," Carter said. "In the car that is."

She looked him up and down. "What exactly are you saying?"

Good question. He wanted to get her back in his bed. That was as clear to him as glass. But even when Jade danced with him in the club, her "I'm not going back there with you" vibes were equally clear.

Carter cleared his throat. "I'm saying that I want in…" He dropped his eyes low, caressing her face, her throat, the slope of her shoulders without laying a hand on her. "I hope you want the same thing."

This woman brought something out in him. Carter

could sense it, and it rose in him as dark and hot and needy. Settled in his teeth and his body like an ache that could only be relieved by one thing. This was like nothing he had felt with her before.

It was strange enough to make him uncomfortable, and uncomfortably hard.

Silver moonlight fell over Jade's face as she watched him, unsmiling. Her face was smooth, soft looking—and damn, did he want to touch—but she also looked tired.

"Carter, the last time I let you *in*—" she gave the last word the same significance he did "—things didn't work out. You hurt me." Then she bit her lip, like she'd said more than she wanted to.

Jade stepped closer to the car and it chirped as it unlocked. She opened the door, got in, leaving one elegant high-heeled foot on the pavement. Reaching across the car, she opened the glove compartment then took out her phone. After sending off a quick text, she more or less gave him her complete attention.

Her lashes fell low over her eyes, hiding her emotions from him. "It was nice to meet your brothers, Carter. That's the only personal thing I can say. Right now, I'm here to work with you. That's all."

She moved to shut the car door and shut him out, and Carter panicked. His grabbed the edge of the door.

"An hour!" He felt like he shouted it, his heart beating much too fast. He couldn't let her walk away again, not when this chance had come to him like some kind of miracle. "That's all I ask. One hour of your time. Tonight."

The refusal was on her face. He could see it as clearly as the flick of her tongue across her bottom lip.

"All right," she said.

What? But his brain quickly caught up. "When? Where?"

"At my hotel." She gave him the address. "Come in an hour, and don't be late."

Before he could respond, she started the car, tucked her high-heeled foot in the sleek machine and drove away. Literally leaving him in the dust.

Come in an hour, and don't be late.

Her words rang like church bells in his head, impossible to ignore.

When he got back to the table, his brothers didn't waste any time.

"So what's up with you and Jade?" Leo asked, faking a predatory look. "Do I have a chance?"

Wolfe, fending off yet another waitress who wasn't even supposed to be taking care of their section, laughed. "You know what's up with him and Jade." He leaned forward, eyes sparkling with wicked humor. "What I don't know is, how did this happen so soon. You just met the woman today."

Wolfe had married Nichelle, his friend and business partner, after years of flirting and dancing around each other. To him, a day was nothing, hell, he probably thought Kingsley's fiancée of three months didn't know his brother enough for marriage either.

"Wait..." Leo frowned over his whiskey. "Is she the girl you knew in college? The one you've been obsessed with for pretty much ten years now?"

"What? What are you talking about?" No way was

he that transparent. And how could Leo know about any so-called obsession when Carter was just now aware of it himself?

"Seriously? That's her?" Wolfe looked the way Jade had gone with a wry smile. "She's nothing like I thought she'd be. From what you said, I expected somebody like Alice. Young-acting and all sunshine and butterflies. This woman will eat you alive." He looked impressed.

"Let's back up here." Carter held up his hands in surrender, looking at his brothers like they were crazy. Because really, that was the only explanation. "What are you all talking about? I never told you about any 'obsession' with a woman."

Leo almost fell out of the booth laughing. His teeth flashed and he honest to God grabbed his stomach. "Yeah, maybe when you're not tired as hell from two or three days straight of work and not trying to keep up your big and bad reputation."

"Yup," his other brother, traitor that he was, chimed in. "When you're tired or when we ask about some girl or other, all you basically say is *She's no Jade* or something like that. Honestly, we were worried you'd never find this woman and find the closure or whatever you need to keep going with your life."

Carter slumped in the chair, the music throbbing around him and his brothers going on with their conversation like they hadn't just dropped a bombshell all over his life. All these years, he thought he'd been playing it cool.

Come in an hour, and don't be late.

He glanced quickly down at his watch, glad the address she'd given him was less than ten minutes from the club. His breath rattled in his chest.

Yes, he dreamed about Jade, but he never compared other women to her. Did he?

No other woman affected him enough to even think of them in the same world as her.

He had his needs. And he took care of them as often as his work with the family would let him. But what they said just didn't make sense.

"You guys are full of it," he finally bit out after a gulp of whiskey.

Leo let out a bark of laughter. "Maybe so, but you're the one in denial."

Goddamn.

Ten years. And this was what he'd been waiting for? Like Wolfe had done before, he looked at the route Jade had taken out of the club and to her sexy little car. Next time he saw his troublemaking brother, he was going to buy Jaxon a meal or at least whatever flavor ice cream he was into at the moment. Jade Tremaine was back in his life, and his blinders were off. He wanted her, and maybe with the help of the IPO offering that he never really supported, he would get her right back where she belonged. With him.

"Okay," he said. And even to his own ears, he sounded dazed.

Wolfe cursed out a laugh. "Damn, brother! It's about time you actually knew what was going on in your own heart."

Yeah. It was about time.

But how could Carter know his own heart when it had only belonged to his family this whole time?

* * *

Carter knocked on Jade's hotel room door, not sure of what he would say. On the ride over, he'd rehearsed a thousand different things, but not one of them seemed right in the end. Before he was ready, the door opened in front of him.

Jade's eyes widened when they saw him. "Nice flowers."

"Nice room." *Nice room? Really? That's all you got?* But he refused to backpedal. "Can I come in?"

"Of course, since you came all this way. And with flowers too." She stepped aside and waved him into the generic but classically luxurious hotel suite. "Unless that bouquet isn't for me." Amusement threaded her voice.

"Who else would it be for?" He looked around, noting the open door of the bedroom and the rolling suitcase sitting on top of the bed.

"I don't know," Jade said from behind him. "Maybe you like to walk around with accessories to tease all the women you pass."

She'd changed from what she'd been wearing at the bar. Now a simple white dress flowed over her subtle curves. She'd showered too. The scent of a mouthwatering combination of spices emanated from her skin. Jade literally smelled like something he wanted to eat.

Carter shifted the flowers, a colorful explosion of red, white and yellow roses already in a clear vase, from one hand to the other. "While I do look good carrying these around, is there anyplace in here I can rest them for a little while?"

A spark of humor caught in her eyes before she

turned away to point at a table near the shuttered window. "You can put them here. They can get some light in the morning."

"Thanks." He put the flowers where she wanted, but once his hands were empty, he stood in the middle of the hotel suite, everything he'd rehearsed stripped from his brain. But at least he wasn't stuttering out empty words.

A sound of impatience fluttered through the room. Hers.

"What did you want to talk to me about, Carter?"

Talk?

Oh, yeah. Right. He cleared his throat and, unbuttoning his suit jacket, claimed one of the armchairs in the little sitting area. He nearly breathed a sigh of relief when she followed him.

"I want to clear the air between us," he said. That sounded like a good enough start.

All around the room were small signs of her having been there for a good little while, a day or three. A handbag in the middle of the small coffee table. Papers neatly stacked next to it. A light jacket thrown across the back of one of the chairs.

"I think you said enough in your office earlier." She sank into the chair opposite him and crossed her long legs. Unable to help it, his eyes flickered down to follow the movement. Miles of smooth brown skin. Legs he'd once felt wrapped around him. Did she have any underwear on?

He winced, disappointed by his wandering thoughts. No, this wasn't what this visit was about.

"No. I didn't say nearly enough. The...situation

caught me off guard. We didn't get to talk, not really. We just threw words at each other before you walked out."

"And you know this time will be different?"

"Yes." It had to be. Carter drew a deep breath and braced his elbows on his spread thighs. "I want you to know what happened to me ten years ago."

"Oh, I know what happened." Her eyes narrowed, like she was staring into some murky pit. "You got what you wanted from a stupid college girl and then you left." She shrugged like it was no big deal. Just another virginity plucked in a college dorm room.

Carter clenched his jaw until it hurt. Of course, she wouldn't make this easy for him. There was nothing for him to do but spit it out. "When you and I were having sex for the first time, my father had a heart attack."

She stiffened across from him, her red-painted mouth hanging slightly open. "Oh my God, Carter…"

"When you left to go back to your dorm, I checked my phone and got the news from my mother." Guilt had torn him apart. There he'd been, buried deeply in the woman he'd wanted his whole college life while his father was barely holding on to his actual life. Listening to his mother's voice-mail message, Carter thought he was going to be sick. But he'd only spared a moment to shower the smell of sex from his skin before jumping on a plane back to Miami.

"My father was in intensive care when I got back home. The rest of the family was there. My mother, my brothers, my sisters. None of us left his side until we were sure he'd make it. For a while, we just didn't know how it would go." Even now, it made him nauseous to think how close he'd come to losing his father. Carter linked his fingers together and pressed them against his chin. "I was in a daze for a while. I know you called. I know you left messages, but I could barely answer to my own name much less have a phone conversation. I didn't want to see a phone. All I wanted to do was give all of my energies and prayers to my father and my family." He lifted his eyes to Jade. "And although I don't regret the choices I made then, I'm sorry I hurt you."

Leaning toward him, she looked shell-shocked. "I… I had no idea."

"I know. And you should have. At least if I'd made the time to call and let you know what was going on, you would know that I…valued what happened between us. Not just the sex, but all of it. All those years we spent getting to know each other, every movie night, every confidence we shared." He paused. "And it means something to me that you chose to give me your virginity."

She jerked like she'd been electrocuted. "I didn't—"

Carter felt an unexpected spike of amusement and he raised an eyebrow in her direction.

Her gaze dropped and he practically felt the scald of embarrassment rising from her cheeks. "I didn't realize you knew I was a virgin."

"I knew," he rumbled back at her.

Carter had heard the rumors Jade's college boyfriend spread around campus, that she was frigid and couldn't stand to be touched, that she didn't even want to be close to any guy. But that wasn't the warm and vibrant girl he knew. When she'd come to him, that irresistible mixture of temptation and vulnerability, his schoolboy willpower was no match to her allure and soft cries of *Please, Carter. Please...* as she kissed his throat and clawed away the buttons of his shirt.

The spots of blood she left behind on his sheets had been small, but they had been very much there.

Still looking embarrassed, Jade jumped up from her chair. The dress fluttered around her legs from her frantic movement. "I didn't know about your father. I..." She shook her head and raked trembling fingers over her sleek, low-cut hair. "I would've understood if only I'd known."

"I know," Carter said.

And that stark fact haunted him every night when he closed his eyes to sleep. By the time he woke up from the fog his father's heart attack and thankful recovery had left him in and returned to campus, it had been too late. Jade was gone. No one would tell him where she went, and by that time she was the one not returning any phone calls.

There had been something else too. Something that shamed him now.

After all those years of wanting Jade—of imagining what it would be like to have the girl who lit up all his days with her smiles and all his nights with fantasies that left him weak and shouting out her name in the aftermath of his sexual release—he'd been simply and terrifyingly afraid.

While waiting and praying with the rest of the family, he found out the secret that most of his siblings apparently already knew. That their mother had cheated on their father, and left him, left all the children. She came back to them eventually. But if a couple he thought would never break apart was so fragile in reality, then what did that mean for any relationship he got in?

Afterward, he realized how stupid he'd been.

Framed against the pale curtains, Jade stood watching him. Light flowed over her face but her expression was closed and unreadable.

What are you thinking now? he wanted to ask her. But she'd probably sooner jab him in the kidneys than give him a straight answer. Instead, he stood up and went to her.

"It might be too late for anything, even forgiveness, between us but that's what I wanted to tell you. I don't want to keep any more secrets between us." Unease flicked at the back of his brain. A memory of his fear. A deeper reason why he hadn't tried harder to reach her that long week they'd waited to see if his father would pull through. "Jade." Carter stepped closer, his hands down at his sides. "Is it too late for you to forgive me?"

She clasped her arms tightly over her chest. "After all this time, it probably doesn't really matter. I..."

Of course, he couldn't forget how she came at him earlier in Kingsley's office. The blatant lie she told about her virginity. She wanted to push him even farther away. Wanted to punish him. Those were the feelings she'd had for him for years now. He couldn't expect them to change in a lightning's flash.

But he could hope.

"I never wanted to hurt you, Jade. The only thing I ever wanted was to make you happy. After what you said about Hudson and how he cheated on you, all I could think of was how much better I'd treat you. I wanted to show you it was okay to be a virgin and to want to be careful—"

She made a sharp noise, one of self-mockery. "All that care I took with my virginity went up in smoke the second you touched me. I guess I wasn't waiting for anything after all."

"Or you were waiting for it to mean something to the person you shared it with."

"But did it, though?" she asked. "Did it mean anything to you?"

God, how could she doubt it?

Before he'd given his body permission, Carter was stepping forward to claim Jade's hand in his. Her fingers were freezing.

He pulled her close and shuddered in relief when she let him. "I would've given anything for you to be mine and mine alone back in college."

"But we're not in college now, Carter." Jade grabbed his other arm and held tight. They stood there, facing off like two gladiators in the arena. "We're not kids anymore."

"But we don't have to be kids to know what desire is, do we?" His thumb stroked her knuckles.

He heard her breath catch, that sound he'd only heard one other time in his life, when he'd had her in his arms and in his bed.

"Carter, don't." She licked her lips, pupils flaring wide open. Jade tugged her hand from his. Both her palms landed flat on his chest. Her fingernails dug into him through the thin silk shirt.

"Don't what?" He tugged her closer until her heat radiated to him, sinking into his chest and his belly.

"Don't tell you how much I still want you? Don't tell you I've been dreaming about you every night for the past ten years—" Her eyes widened and she made that startled sound again. "Don't confess how much I ache to just kiss you right now?"

And that wasn't even half of what he was feeling. He hoped for now, though, what he'd said to her was enough.

"You don't play fair," Jade gasped a moment before she kissed him. Her soft mouth pressed into his and that was all the permission Carter needed. He parted his lips and took what she offered.

She tasted like longing. And, oh, the sound she made. A deep and soft moan that made him realize he was not alone in this. She may have hated him. She may not have wanted to see his face ever again. But she still wanted him. She still ached for him like the afternoon she'd come begging for him to make love to her.

Their tongues twisted together, slick and hot, and he moaned at the scorching pleasure of it. No wonder none of the other women he'd been with had been able to keep his interest. All these years, he'd been waiting to feel THIS again.

Joy. Excitement. Ecstasy, just from the feel of her mouth under his. Panting. Fiery. Needy.

His heart roared in his chest, thudding frantically.

"Carter…" She moaned and twisted against him, soft and scented from her bath and whatever lotion she'd smoothed into her oh-so-soft skin. "I missed you," she moaned. "I missed you so much."

Her desperate words obliterated the last of his doubts. Before he knew it, he had her backed against the curtained window. Even through the thin cloth, he could feel the coolness of the window glass seeping into his flattened palms on either side of her hips. Her thighs moved restlessly against his.

With a groan, he yanked up her dress and slid his fingers between her suddenly parted thighs.

"Jade…" She wasn't wearing anything under that thin white dress. His knees nearly buckled. "Can I have you again?" He gasped the question into her mouth, his fingers already sliding into her wetness. "God, I'd do anything."

Her thighs opening wider, the breath stuttering in her throat like she'd run around Miami and back. "Anything?" Her hips snaked, sucking his fingers deeper inside her.

"Yes!" Carter growled. He barely felt coherent. His body was overheated, ready and so damn hard. He dropped his head forward, trying to get himself back under control. Trying to stop any more pleas from falling out of his mouth.

But she wasn't making it easy for him. "Show me how much you want me," she rasped. "Show me now." Jade rode his fingers, moving her hips sinuously, eagerly.

Carter had never been so jealous of his own fingers in his entire life.

Obviously, he still wasn't thinking clearly. It felt good to tell her what happened years ago. But now his desire for Jade felt like a river that had broken beyond its banks, threatening to wash away everything else in this life. He pulsed with it. His heart, his mind, his…

He pressed the heel of his hand in his lap and drew

a breath. Then her hand was there too, unzipping him and pulling out the long club of his sex through the opening in his pants. The lust flashed through him like his own personal lightning bolt. Sudden, hot and uncontrollable.

"Do you have—" Jade squeezed him with her soft hand and Carter's eyes crossed.

What? Oh. Right. He fumbled in his wallet for a condom, ripped it open and quickly put it on.

She was so open, so beautiful, her smooth legs and entire body spread out against the curtained window glass like a feast for him to devour. Carter had been starving for ten years. With a hoarse shout, he pierced his sex deep into the heart of her.

"Carter!" Jade gasped, clinging to him. "More!" Her legs locked around his hips. Her center clenched around him, and he was lost.

Whatever civilized and cool conversation he'd thought of having with her before was long gone. All that mattered were the desperate movements of her hips against his, the tight heaven of her around him, the bite of her nails in the back of his neck, urging him on.

Gasping, he pulled back and thrust deep into her. Perfection. They both groaned. Desire buzzed down his spine and gathered low between his legs, rocketing him on. Jade trembled against him, breaths and screams knocked from her open mouth with each window-rattling thrust of hips.

"More!" She gripped him tight. Her nails shredded the back of his neck and raked over his scalp.

It hurt but Carter wouldn't have it any other way. He gave her everything he had, tapping again and again on that place inside her that made Jade shudder and wail. The storm gathered hard and fast in him. It was coming, and coming fast. But he didn't want to leave her behind. "Jade, baby…?"

"Yes, Carter, yes!" She threw her head back and screamed even louder than before, her sex a clenching, wet fist around him.

That was the permission he needed to let go. His rhythm faltered, his smooth strokes becoming ragged as he lost himself to the rising orgasm, shouting her name and slamming into her again and again while she and the glass shuddered under him. A white heat blazed through him. His eyes squeezed tightly shut. Then everything went quiet.

It all came back to him in a savage rush. Her pleased sighs. The sound of his gasping breaths. A humming from the room's AC.

Carter's knees trembled. The sweat ran hot under his shirt, down his haunches and thighs. He sagged into the hot line of her throat, hands still braced on the glass and his sex still buried inside her. Slowly, her legs dropped from around his waist.

He could feel her already withdrawing from him in more ways than one. "Jade?"

She shook her head, the regret clouding her eyes. Disappointment fisted in Carter's stomach. Just once, he wished he could get something he wanted without it being tainted by conditions and circumstances he had no control over.

"We can't do this again." She jerked her dress back down and brushed a trembling hand over her face, wiping away the sweat there. "We… I work for your family.

This would be… This is a bad idea. A very bad idea." Jade licked her lips and darted her eyes away, like she was trying to convince herself too.

"Okay." Still reeling from his orgasm, Carter barely stopped himself from firing her on the spot. No, that was unprofessional. He didn't do crap like that. Not ever.

He disposed of the full condom and zipped himself up. The sweat now felt cool again on his skin, and his heartbeat was finally slowing down.

"You should—" Jade began.

"Go," he finished.

"Yes," they said together. That was obviously what she wanted.

Carter backed away from her, his whole body still tingling with the aftermath of his orgasm, but still hungry for hers again.

"We should talk tomorrow," he said, fighting to keep his voice neutral and controlled.

"Or maybe the day after that," Jade countered.

No. He wouldn't let her run away. "Tomorrow," he said firmly.

But Jade only slid him a look from the corners of her eyes and swept toward the door to pull it open. "I'll talk with you soon, Carter," she said, cool and no-nonsense like he just hadn't been buried deep inside her wetness while she begged for him not to stop.

A breeze winged through one of the open windows to flutter the dress around her body and bring the scent of her once again to his nose. His mouth watered. His nostrils flared. But he walked toward the open door to give her the space she demanded.

For now.

Chapter 5

The ground under Jade's feet was so very unsteady when she was with Carter. Everything was uncertain, including how she was supposed to handle this new turn in their relationship, this formerly latent desire that had flared between them last night as if it had never waned.

But she couldn't afford to let it become a thing. They worked together. His family hired her to do a job and no part of that job description included climbing Carter Diallo like a tree.

Now nothing was as simple as it should have been.

It had all started to feel so good, so normal, to be there in the club with him and his brothers, talking about nothing important. As an only child, she'd never had that. The unconditional support of a sibling, the way they sometimes seemed to read each other's minds, the teasing that came naturally and the way they instantly absorbed her into their circle.

Years ago, during one of the times she and Carter *really* talked, he said something she didn't quite understand.

I miss my family, he'd said so matter-of-factly that she'd overlooked it at first.

But then she caught up and couldn't imagine *feeling* that, much less saying it out loud. Her parents were her only family. They came to see her nearly every month and they went out to dinner at whatever place her father wanted to try. Jade never got the chance to miss them. But, more important, she *wanted* to miss them. She wanted that ache of homesickness that many of her new friends talked about.

For her, though, college had only been a chance to escape from her family's rigid control and the ignorance they'd imprisoned her with. Because of them, she'd known nothing about the real world. Nothing about sex, independence or even normal interpersonal relationships.

What man named his wife's child after his mistress?

No, Jade had never missed her parents after they let her go. She never longed for her so-called family.

But Carter had been unhappy without his. And now she could see why.

If she had a family like the Diallos, she'd miss them too.

With her most businesslike face on, she opened the door to her parents' house.

"Come in, gentlemen."

Jaxon and Carter Diallo took up the space in front of

the door. Carter in his usual suit, a gray one this time that looked like it matched her car, and the young boy genius in designer dark wash jeans and a pale yellow dress shirt rolled up at the elbows.

They were identically handsome, she tried to tell herself objectively. But the boy Jaxon didn't hold a candle to the magnetic and masculine strength of his brother, a grown man. Jade only allowed herself one quick and guilt-free look before stepping back to allow them inside the house. She had to be professional.

She had to pretend Carter hadn't been in her hotel room last night, hadn't made love to her, hadn't made her doubt…everything.

Despite promising herself to not do any work before seven a.m., she'd sent emails to the Diallo lawyer and then to Jaxon Diallo himself, requesting a meeting on neutral ground to discuss what they needed to do. She didn't feel like exposing herself to those ridiculous feelings again by going back to the Diallo building, but she also needed to make them know she was the one making the plays here.

So she set up a meeting for eleven in the morning at her parents' house. A local catering service arranged late-morning coffee and an early lunch in the empty second floor of the house. The small dining room table and chairs, sofa and a coffee table Jade had brought upstairs took up only the smallest amount of room in the otherwise empty space. But she needed it to be workable, not pretty.

"Head on upstairs and to your right. You'll see the table set up as soon as you get there."

"What the hell is this?" Jaxon started up as he

looked around, his steps slow through the foyer despite the incentive of Carter's intimidating form crowding him from behind. "We couldn't meet at the office?"

"This *is* an office," Jade said with an eyebrow pointedly raised. "Mine."

She didn't stay to watch them walk up. In the kitchen, she took a few sips of fortifying breath before heading after them.

When she got upstairs, she found Jaxon looking over the railing and down to the covered pool while Carter prowled around the vast space with a frown between his brows. He looked up as soon as she came in, eyes fastened completely on her. She couldn't help but shiver from the way he raked her entire body with his eyes and although she wore a simple sheath dress and medium-height heels, his look made her feel as if she was wearing something much more revealing. Not just of her body, but of her heart and soul too.

This was ridiculous, she thought. And none of this fanciful thinking was going to get her anywhere good. With a click of her heels against the tile floors, she turned sharply away from him.

"Thanks for coming on such short notice," she said.

"As if I had a choice," Jaxon muttered.

God, was this boy going to be pouting all day?

He strolled in from the balcony, looking between her and Carter with an eerily perceptive look on his face. "What's up with you two? You look guilty, like you're hiding secrets."

While the caterers, two women who came quietly in, settled the carafes of coffee and small pastries in the middle of the table, Jaxon roamed the large room. He looked bored.

"This is a nice place. A little empty. The owners could put some money into fixing it up, though."

He looked at Jade like he was being a smart-ass, convinced she was the owner.

"They're dead," she said.

Technically, she was the owner but she was getting rid of it as soon as humanly possible. Why mention the intermediate step?

"Sit down and stop being an ass, Jaxon." Carter appeared in Jade's line of sight again, sleek and gorgeous in a designer suit.

As if she could ever stop being aware of him.

She threw him a sour look. "Thanks, Carter. But I think Jaxon and I are doing just fine."

"This is your definition of *fine*, huh?" Jaxon made a scornful noise. "I'd hate to see what you think is a disaster."

She shrugged and settled down at the head of the table, letting the young man know in no uncertain terms who was in charge of this meeting. He didn't sit down but continued to hover in the room, going from blank space to blank space like he was searching for something when it was obvious he was only doing it to piss Jade off. Or bide his time for something she had no idea about.

"The disaster is this mess that you landed your family in."

He flashed a look filled with fury and contempt. "My family? No, this is just *my* own mess. And it isn't even that much of a mess. Nessa is pissed at me, and she's trying to set the world against me because of it. But it'll all blow over. It's nothing."

"If only that were true." She opened her folder and slid a piece of paper to where she'd invited Jaxon to sit, ignoring the fact that he was nowhere near the chair. "The world at large is eating up Nessa's story. Everyone with an opinion thinks you stole her app and stole her chance for a better life. You're the villain here, along with your family for supporting you."

"That's stupid," Jaxon hissed, all defiance.

He was very young, Jade thought. And remembered what she had been like at that age. A fool. Alone.

She hid the sudden tremor behind an impatient-sounding breath. "I'm not sure whether or not your family let you know what's going on, but because the Diallo Corporation is going public, it can't afford any scandal. Nothing. And the fact that you messed this girl up enough for her to want to ruin you—"

"Any idiot can just look at our profiles and résumés and see what the hell is really going on. She doesn't have a leg to stand on."

"Unfortunately, the only idiots who'll react strongly are the ones who want to nail you to the wall." And just a few minutes in Jaxon's company and Jade wanted to slap him.

He was arrogant, unrepentant and street-smart. It wasn't just the way he dressed and the air of entitlement he carried around with him, it was the frightening intelligence in his eyes, the obviously muscular and fit body, the way he stripped you down with his eyes, not caring that he was making a person feel like a commodity to be used and discarded instead of a human being. None of that would get him any sympathy in any court of public opinion.

"Carter, what do you think?" Jade asked.

She looked at Carter who she suddenly realized had been watching her the whole time. He stood nearly in the center of the room, his arms crossed over his powerful chest. She cleared her throat to loosen the frog that had suddenly taken up residence there.

She deliberately turned her back on Jaxon who had wandered over to the desk to look with disdain through the papers—photos of the girl he'd had sex with and then abandoned, screenshots of the tweets she'd sent out accusing Jaxon of stealing her app, a selection of the supportive responses she'd gotten on social media, including a tweet from a major local paper.

"You don't care what I think," Carter said with a careless shrug that told Jade it didn't bother him. And about this, he was so very right.

If he'd known what to do, she wouldn't be here.

"Do what you need to do," he finished up in his growling voice.

"You two couldn't be more obvious if you tried." Jaxon interrupted their staring contest. Seated now at the table, he rolled his eyes.

His phone chimed once, then a moment later, Carter's did too. Carter ignored his but Jaxon took his phone and unlocked the screen.

"Nice." For a second, his face was more than just the petulance of a spoiled child. "Kingsley and Adah will finally finish up the longest engagement in history next month."

"We already have the wedding on the family calendar," Carter said.

Jaxon grinned down at this phone as he tapped out a text. "Yeah, but it felt like it was taking forever to get here."

Why did Jade feel like she'd lost control of the entire meeting?

"This is the reminder about the engagement party," Jaxon said.

"Again, we know all that."

"Do you know it's next week?" Jaxon challenged his older brother with a smirk.

Carter's face didn't change, but Jade got the feeling that he had forgotten. Maybe his assistant didn't send him a reminder memo with the rest of his morning messages.

"Anyway, I'm pumped," Jaxon said with a surprisingly sweet grin. "I'm glad Kingsley has a woman he can love almost as much as he loves the company. Adah is nice."

"Yes, she is," Carter quietly agreed.

Jaxon turned to Jade with a glint of mischief in his eyes. "You should come to the engagement party, as Carter's date. Wouldn't that be something?"

Again, Carter's face didn't so much as twitch, but Jade was willing to bet he felt far from brotherly toward Jaxon in that moment.

"All right, let's finish up here then so you can go back to your family business."

Jade clapped her hands once and nearly smiled when both men looked at her with varying degrees of surprise. Which is to say that Carter just looked at her.

"This meeting is basically a courtesy, Jaxon," she said. "I have a few strategies I want to put in place, including using newspaper articles, social media posts and other things to make you look like not quite an ass."

"I work hard on this ass, thanks very much." He smirked and turned to flex his glutes at Jade.

"That I don't need to know." Jade bit off the words. "I'll have some people start cleaning up your social media image, deleting old tweets, things like that. In the meantime, try to act like a nice kid instead of... What you are?"

"A nineteen-year-old genius on the board of a multibillion-dollar company, who has his own successful app also making money and who happens to like sex with a variety of women?"

He had the nerve to act like it was a real question, his eyebrow going up, head leaned toward her like he was waiting for an answer.

"Or like an entitled ass."

"Okay, then."

"Cooperate with my people or I will make you cooperate with them. From now on, your social media accounts are being managed by me and my team. I'll send over a couple of reporters to interview you about your college choices—" he'd gotten into Massachusetts Institute of Technology, Harvard, Yale, as well as a small college in Miami, but hadn't announced his decision yet other than to say he wanted to defer admission for a year "—and try to be nice. Just in case though, I'll have someone there to give you pointers on niceness." It wasn't going to be her.

"You should totally take her to the engagement party, Carter," Jaxon said, his pale eyes glinting with mischief and something else Jade couldn't read. "The family would totally love her."

They thankfully finished up the meeting a few minutes later. Jaxon practically ran out the door, leaving Jade and Carter alone in the heavy silence.

"You know, I actually don't think that's a bad idea."

"What?" Jade narrowed her gaze at him.

"For you to come with me and meet the family." The corner of his mouth twitched. "I promise they won't bite."

She opened her mouth to tell him *no way*, but he raised a quick hand.

"If you come to the party, you'll get to see what we're about. Not just the dynamic between me and the rest of the sibs, but the company mentality too."

It didn't really make any sense. She could do her job just as well, maybe even better, if she kept her distance from Carter and his beautiful and intimidatingly huge family.

But don't you want to know more about him?

The dangerous voice that had ended up throwing her in bed and under him in the first place whispered at her. And she couldn't deny she was curious what made him the guy he was in college as well as the man who stood before her now.

She licked her lips, knowing before she spoke what she was going to say.

"Why not? Let's do it."

What could it hurt?

Chapter 6

On the afternoon of the engagement party, Jade stepped out into the lobby of the South Beach Ritz-Carlton and found Carter exactly where he said he'd be waiting for her.

At first, she offered to meet him at the house where the party was supposed to be, but he'd refused, saying it would be strange for him not to at least pick her up. It seemed like a transparent play to come back to her hotel, but she gave in. It wasn't that serious, and in the end, it wouldn't matter. Yes, they'd ended up in bed together. That was in the past, though. It was never going to happen again.

But damn, did he have to look so good?

Seated in one of the plush chairs in the lobby, he looked effortlessly attractive in yet another one of his suits. This one was a blue pinstripe, perfectly cut to his muscular body. His big feet looked elegant and capable in a pair of saddle-brown monk straps.

If she hadn't been paying such close attention, she might have missed the way other people—men and women—looked at him. He was so comfortable in his skin, elegant and…large, an ankle crossed at the knee to show off the gleam of his shoes and the mouthwatering muscularity of his thighs and calves. Unlike most of the people in the lobby already waiting, he wasn't looking at any sort of electronic device. Just watching the people around him from beneath half-lowered lashes. When he spotted her, he rose easily to his feet.

Jade, like the rest of the room, she suspected, drew an admiring breath.

Good Lord. He was like a dream come true. A man tall and broad enough to protect and shelter a woman, and who looked good in a suit. Good enough to eat.

Her eyelashes fluttered down as she remembered that she had gotten a taste of him. And just how delicious it had been. But they couldn't go there again.

"You look nice." He looked her up and down, a subtle movement of his eyes. The warmth in them grew when he swept his gaze down for a second look.

Although she wasn't quite sure about the crowd—what the hell were you supposed to wear to an engagement party anyway?—she felt relatively safe in the sleeveless burgundy dress. It hugged her body, but wasn't too tight, and gave her legs just enough freedom of movement in case she had to run like hell out of there.

Hey, she didn't know what she was going to be walking into.

"Thank you." She walked the last few feet toward him in the four-inch designer heels her assistant back in San Diego had picked out. "You don't look so bad yourself."

"I bet you say that to all your fake dates." His tone was dry.

She didn't bother replying to that foolishness. "I hope you weren't waiting too long."

"No, you're right on time, as usual," Carter said. "I just like getting to a place early."

"So you can catch people by surprise?"

He shrugged, a resettling of that elegant suit on his perfect frame. "Nope, unless it's work, I'm not that interested in other people's reactions."

The thing was she knew why. As much as she felt he'd changed since college—and yet somehow was still the same in some ways—he was the one who always liked to sit and take things in. He hated to rush.

She remembered that about him, even when they'd made their friend dates to watch movies. When she got to the lounge with the TV, he would always be already there, just sitting and drinking the world in.

Quiet. Gorgeous. Unaware of his beauty. Or even his strength back then.

"Where did you park?" Jade asked.

"With the valet." He gestured ahead of him toward the front doors of the hotel.

They made their way out to the valet's station.

"That was fast," the kid said with with a sinking expression. Like he was sad Carter was back so soon.

"My date was just as early as I was," Carter said

with an unsmiling look that somehow managed to convey a kind of warmth.

The kid spared Jade a brief but appreciative glance before calling another green-suited valet over. "Watch the stand, I'm getting his car." He jerked his head toward Carter and grabbed the keys before the other boy could do more than sputter and frown.

"Do you come to this hotel often?" That was the only explanation she could think of for them to practically fawn over Carter like that.

"Is that the retro pickup line the cool kids are using these days?"

She ran back through what she'd just said and nearly bit her tongue clean through. She poked his side, then immediately regretted it. "You know that's not what I mean." Then she realized again what she'd just done. Treated him like they were still in college and were kids together with the same things on their minds, the same trajectory, the same understood desires.

But Carter remained expressionless, only the tiniest tic of movement at the corner of his mouth betraying his awareness of what just happened. "I can only take you at face value. Isn't that what you said?"

She could've kicked him in the shins if she wasn't above such things. Just then, a car pulled up near the front steps where they stood. An electric-blue Bugatti Chiron with windows tinted so dark it had to be illegal even for Florida.

The car was absolutely gorgeous. A model Jade had admired before at car shows but never thought was a fit for her. She much preferred her cooler English ride, but this car was all power and quiet opulence from hood to bumper. A car made not just to be looked at—because *damn*, it was fine—but also to be driven. Her palms itched just gazing at it.

She opened her mouth to say how delicious it was. Then remembered that Carter wasn't a friend, only a colleague and a reluctant one at that. The door opened and the valet jumped out. His smile looked big enough to light up a small planet. He practically floated across the asphalt to open the passenger-side door of the car.

He beamed at Carter. "Here you are, sir."

Only a clench of her jaw stopped Jade's mouth from dropping open. The Carter she'd known before would have never…

"Thank you." Carter passed the kid a twenty dollar bill.

Still in shock mode, Jade walked toward the door but stopped still when Carter slid into the passenger seat and closed the door in her face. He slid down the window and arched an eyebrow at Jade.

"You want to drive, right?"

She nearly tripped over her own two feet dashing over to driver's side. Her heart thumped loud and hard as she slid into the plush leather seat, instantly overcome by the scent of new leather, new car and the spicy aftershave of the man seated next to her. But she firmly closed the driver's side door and tried to play it off as best as she could.

"So where are we going?" she asked.

Her fingers curved around the leather-wrapped steering wheel without her permission and she may have been just a little bit breathless.

"Make a left out of here and head toward the highway." The laughter in Carter's voice let her know just how transparent she was.

She took off and just about wet herself from how smoothly the car shifted, how sweetly it took even the little side road. Maybe she should ask for the car as her fee instead of actual money. But even as she thought it, she dismissed it. Carter belonged with this car, this new version of Carter anyway. Just like she belonged with hers. The thought strangely disappointed her for a moment before the exhilaration of driving brought the pleasure pulsing deliciously through her fingertips, into her body, down to her feet as she shifted gears and headed in the direction he indicated. They took a few small streets before they finally got onto the highway.

"Now, drive until I tell you when you get off," he rumbled.

She sneaked a peek at him to see if he was just being funny but he was as calm and expressionless as ever.

"Very smooth," he complimented after a few moments. His gaze on her legs felt like a heated caress.

After minimal direction from him and barely any conversation, they pulled up to a high steel gate in Coconut Grove. A remote opened the gates and a long and elegant drive took them up to a large house. It looked too homey to be a mansion but was much too large to be a mere "house."

"Here we are," he said. "Just park next to any of these other cars and make sure we have room to get out if you need to leave early."

She may have been raised an only child, but she damn sure wasn't going to ask him to leave a family event just because she felt out of place. She could be an ass but not that much of one.

The large circular driveway already had nearly a dozen cars parked there. They ran the gamut from Honda to Mini Cooper all the way to a Koenigsegg Trevita. Jade couldn't help but gawk at all the gorgeous cars as she slowly and carefully cruised past, looking for a place to park Carter's precious baby.

Yes, she knew his family was rich. The numbers were all there when she'd checked over Diallo Corporation and its board members and officers who also happened to be members of one large family. But the house—grand without being ostentatious—the cars, Jaxon's casual disregard for any other pleasure but his own, gave her the idea this was wealth she hadn't really seen from up close before.

Not that she was going to let it intimidate her.

Jade parked the Bugatti and leaned back in the seat to enjoy a few minutes of quiet in the after-silence of the engine. She licked her lips and couldn't stop herself from smiling, no matter how much she told herself it wasn't a good idea. Or whatever.

"Your car is delicious." A complete and utter understatement, although she would eat the little blue beast up if she could.

"Thank you. Did you enjoy the drive?"

What kind of question was that? She turned to him with an eyebrow up and incredulity in her face only to see his smile. She smiled back at him.

"Yes, yes, I did. Thanks for sharing."

"Anytime," he said.

The word throbbed in the car between them long

after Carter finished speaking. This could become a habit. She fought against the childhood practice of lip-biting that had plagued her all the way through her freshman year of college.

Jade cleared her throat. "Ready?"

"Of course." After a last look at her, significant and heavy, Carter got out of the car.

A swift breath later, Jade followed him and closed the door behind her. It shut with a firm sound she felt all the way through her body. She rolled her shoulders back at the loveliness of it. Fingers clenched around the key fob, she forced herself to hand it to Carter once she stepped over to his side of the car.

"You hold on to it. We're leaving here together later, after all."

She slid the key fob into her purse with a small frisson of satisfaction. "That's not fair," she said.

"What do you mean?" He started toward the wide stairs of the veranda and she fell into step beside him.

He was playing her, stroking her good side but she had no idea why. It was so obvious that it was almost laughable. But he didn't crack so much as a smile.

"God, Carter. You are no good at this subterfuge stuff, are you?"

He only shook his head. "Come on, let me introduce you to my family and the happy couple."

While they strolled up the elegant veranda with tropical plants lining the graceful railing and trailing green and luxurious up the white columns, he explained that his brother met Adah when he was in Aruba on one of his escapes from family life.

Escapes? She watched his face as he talked, thought

she caught a hint of something like envy in the strong lines of his jaw and full mouth.

"Does he get to escape often?" she asked, because it seemed something worth asking.

"Once a year around the same time."

"And what about you? Do you get to escape like the CEO of Diallo Corporation?" She thought she knew the answer.

It was in the way he had so quickly and capably taken on every responsibility within sight, even those he didn't need to. It was in what they called him, The Magic Man, out there in the world. He was damn near a legend out there in terms of what he could accomplish in the name of his family.

She knew plenty of headhunters and companies who'd give up at least a million in assets just to have him work for them, hell, to have him for an afternoon. He made problems disappear, sometimes even before they started.

"I don't really have time for that," he said in response to her question.

Jade nodded. Of course.

"You should think about a vacation," she said softly. "If the CEO can take off every year at the same time, you should be able to, as well."

"The company doesn't work like that," he said. "Or at least I don't."

The wide front door opened and they stepped inside to a chaos of voices and laughter. Nothing at all like a mansion. She heard children, adults; she heard music. From far off she thought she detected pots clanging.

"Carter!"

A whirlwind with big cottony hair flung herself at him. "I was waiting for you to come."

The whirlwind wasn't a child exactly. The lack of childhood roundness was hard to miss in the beautiful face, as was the fox-like intelligence that seemed common to the Diallo family. But the unabashed enthusiasm, the eagerness to show love, was innocent and sweet and Jade couldn't help but smile.

"Who are you, anyway?" The pixie looked up at Jade from her octopus-type grip around Carter's waist. Definitely not innocent or childlike.

But Jade didn't allow her smile to fade at the confrontational tone. "I'm a friend."

"Don't be rude, Elia," Carter said at the same time, but he curved his large hand protectively around the pixie's shoulder.

"I'm not being rude, I'm being direct." Elia pulled herself from Carter just enough to put out a hand for Jade to shake. "I'm Elia Diallo. What's your name?"

Jade gave her own name and watched with shock as the suspicion transformed to a look of pleased surprise. "Cool!"

What was this about?

Carter shook his head. "Don't you have something else to do?" he asked, mock irritation in his tone.

But Elia shook her head. "Nope. The only thing I have on my agenda is to harass my favorite brother."

Then Carter actually laughed. While they'd been talking, Jade noticed a few people throwing them curious looks.

Well, at least they weren't giving her the side-eye.

"Come on in," Elia said. "You know Mama's been

waiting for you to get here." She threw her arms around both of their waists, putting herself firmly in the middle.

The house was packed. Servants uniformed in elegant black and white moved silently among the endless supply of beautiful people perched everywhere Jade looked. She and Carter moved through the sitting room—where no one was actually sitting—to a long and wide hallway decorated with family photographs, most of them with laughing and smiling people, with some sprinkling of art pieces here and there, out to the backyard.

The air left Jade's lungs in a rush.

The backyard was like a place from a fairy tale. Wide and long, with a garden on one side separated from the rest of the yard by a smooth iron fence, nothing sharp to accidentally hurt the little ones, and filled with every kind of blooming flower imaginable. The scent was intoxicating, even in the relatively crisp October air. Far back and at the end of the cobblestoned walkway was a tall gazebo, white and lacey, that looked like it had come from a storybook. Bright pink bougainvillea wound around its railings and up to its peaked top.

A couple danced in the gazebo, swaying to the old-fashioned Jamaican music coming from the speakers. They danced closely together, a sensual movement in the faintly cool breeze. Their laughter poured down the winding path and settled into Jade's ears.

Off to the side but closer to the house was a pool. It was fenced off and covered in a way that the pools of most Florida homes with children were. It looked more like a greenhouse, brilliant as it was with more flowers, than an everyday structure that happened to have a swimming pool inside.

Even though there had been a lot of people in the house, this was apparently where most of the Diallos were. They were so beautiful that they fit in perfectly with the fairy-tale backyard.

"It's nice, isn't it?" Elia said with a pleased grin. "Kingsley's best friend, Victor, designed it. That man is a genius!"

"Who's a genius?"

A gorgeous woman in bright yellow swam through the ocean of beautiful people to kiss Carter on the cheek and hug him as much as Elia's clench would allow. The pixie surprised Jade by releasing her and Carter when the woman hugged and kissed her too.

"Your husband," Elia said. "I was just telling Jade that Victor designed the backyard."

"Ah, yes." The woman grinned, showing off pretty white teeth and a smile that must have melted hearts and boxer briefs all across Miami. "He *is* amazing."

The look on her face said she was absolutely sincere in her statement. She cast a look over her shoulder as if searching for said amazing husband. She must have seen him because she blew a kiss somewhere across the yard. Jade didn't see any answering kisses being blown or even one of those cheesy catch-kiss motions —did people even do that outside middle school?— so she didn't get the chance to see this singular speci-men for herself.

Then the woman moved to Carter's other side where it just so happened that Jade stood. "I'm Mella." She warmly grasped Jade's hands in hers, her expressive eyes actually twinkling. "Welcome to the family."

What? "Oh! I'm not—"

But Mella was already moving away, sailing toward where she'd blown her kiss.

Then Kingsley came out of nowhere with a familiar woman who would've stopped traffic in any crowd. His fiancée who'd visited him the other day at his office.

After greeting his pixie sister with a warm kiss on each cheek, which made her giggle, he gave Carter's shoulder a friendly squeeze. "Good to see you before the crowd got too intense," Kingsley said.

Damn, what would it be like once it got really *intense*? This army of gorgeous people was enough to make anyone nervous. And by anyone, she just meant her.

Kingsley gave Carter one last squeeze before turning his charm and a warm hand clasp onto Jade. "And it's good to see you again, Ms. Tremaine."

"I told you to call me Jade." She didn't see the harm in the friendly lie.

"Jade, then." He pulled his fiancée closer. "Obviously, you guys remember my fiancée, Adah."

They hadn't formally met but Jade would never forget such a face, figure and smile. Adah was beautiful, but her beauty came as much from the fact that she didn't seem to know just how gorgeous she was. Enviable body, warm smile, a dimple in the center of her stubborn-looking chin and a face straight from the pages of a magazine.

The corners of Adah's pretty eyes crinkled. "Hi there. I know we weren't introduced. Don't let Kingsley turn you into a head case. He'll have you thinking his suggestions are yours if you're not too careful." She reached in for a full-body hug and, after a moment's surprise, Jade relaxed in her welcoming embrace. "It's good to officially meet you."

They were a very touchy-feely group. Married into the Diallos or not.

"Congratulations on your engagement," she said to Adah.

"Hey, what about me?" Kingsley asked with a laugh. "Shouldn't I be congratulated on snagging the best woman in the world?"

"The best woman in the world for *you*." A rumbling voice, deep enough to rival Carter's, broke out of the crowd. It was Wolfe, one of the brothers from the club. The pretty one who was married to the love of his life. At least according to what Carter said.

Jade wasn't sure she believed in that kind of love.

"Obviously," Kingsley said. "Otherwise, Adah would have a thousand men all lined up to marry her, plus a few of those studs already in the harem someplace."

"And you already keep me busy," she said with a crooked smile. "I wouldn't know what to do with any more boy toys." Adah patted Kingsley on his impressive chest and grinned. "Unless they can cook. If yes, then sign me up for two."

"Come on, babe. It's the *one* thing I don't do well."

"True," Adah agreed with another pat that morphed into a caress as Jade watched them.

Wolfe made a show of covering his eyes. "Jesus... You must be in love with this fool to think that, Adah."

Jade could see why Adah and her Diallo man were a

perfect fit. Anyone looking at them could see the love between the couple from outer space.

Envy throbbed dully in her chest, but she did her best to ignore it.

Eyes suddenly stinging, she made some excuse and turned away from the group, walking quickly in the direction of the house. On the way there, she grabbed a glass of punch from the tray of a passing waiter. Inside the house, she slipped neatly into a nearly hidden alcove and simply watched.

Everyone looked happy.

Was everyone as happy as they seemed?

And it wasn't even that they all had smiles all over their faces, but it was in the way they held themselves with a kind of contentment Jade hadn't seen in a long time, if ever. The closest thing she could remember like this was in college when many of the girls were unfurling like new buds in the sun after being away from home, away from parents who had sheltered them too long in the dark.

Like Jade's parents.

Those girls had seemed so happy to be alive and away from the shadows of another's influence. Back then it was all illusion because what did eighteen-year-olds know about real repression? Not having your parents allow you to stay out late on a Saturday night wasn't the same thing as being kept away from everything related to sex and growing up and being your own person.

Jade's parents had kept these things from her and she had been too much of a coward, much too afraid to go and seek these things out on her own while away during the school hours of the day.

No, these people, these Diallos looked free in a way she envied.

Jade bit her lip and and turned away.

Across the room, a group of four or five people broke out in applause.

"You should name the baby after me," someone in the group shouted.

More celebration.

Jade turned away from that too, fighting the ache of tears in her throat.

Dammit, she had a reason for being here at this party. And it wasn't to hide behind a potted plant like some pariah in middle school. Carter. She needed to find him.

Most likely, though, he wasn't even where she'd left him. Despite his size, the man moved fast and was in high demand.

For now, the big glass of rum punch she'd downed was catching up with her. She stepped out of her hiding place, ventured outside and tapped a passing waiter.

"Excuse me, can you tell me where the bathroom is?"

The man, handsome in the black-and-white tuxedo uniform that marked the servers as very different from the informally dressed guests, gave her form a brief look and smile before he directed her where to go. Inside the house, of course.

After at least a dozen *excuse mes* and *pardons* she found herself inside the massive house again and wending her way through the wide hallways and to the restroom behind a beautiful, winding staircase. But the door was locked.

Damn.

Getting desperate now that a bathroom was so close but at the same time far away, she looked up the pretty staircase. Maybe there was one at the top of the stairs. Jade quickly slipped up there and found the door a few feet from the landing, unoccupied, thank God, and slipped inside.

Behind the locked door, she relieved her nearly bursting bladder with a heartfelt sigh.

How much punch did I drink anyway? Damn...

After making sure she wasn't about to track any toilet paper out of the bathroom on her heels, she re-touched her makeup.

Sounds of the lively get-together reached her. Laughter. Familiar conversation. She thought she even heard a pair of lovers kissing and murmuring lowly to each other. It all made her feel very apart.

Lonely even, to be honest.

Everyone looked happy, like they were celebrating, and she was there for work. And to feel, once again, apart from everyone else.

God, how pathetic am I? She rolled her eyes at herself then rechecked her face in the mirror.

The same dark eyes and firm mouth. Her expression one of protective coolness, one she was long familiar with. Then, if everything was the same, why did she feel so different?

Something inside her had melted the instant she saw Carter a few days ago. To the very depths of her, she felt more tender, more vulnerable.

Screw that.

Abruptly, she turned away from her reflection.

No, she was *not* that. Not a soft-boiled egg waiting for Carter to come and scoop out her insides and make mush of them again.

Her phone chimed. Nearly sighing with relief, she plucked it out of her purse and looked at the email.

Jade—We have a bit of an emergency there in Miami. Your man, Owen Van Tyle, is on the loose again. Word is he's someplace down there and his wife's not trying to make the news again. Can you handle it?

Jade nearly rolled her eyes. Owen Van Tyle was the trophy husband of a very rich and very beautiful dot-com titan. Despite his less than sexy name, he was handsome and dressed well and knew just the right things to say when a camera was in his face. The problem was that, despite having a millionaire wife who could pass for a supermodel, he had the consistent inability to keep it in his pants.

His wife, Monica Van Tyle, had been a client of Jade's on and off for years. Monica wasn't just a brilliant millionaire, she was also a society darling in San Diego and the daughter of a famous actress. Monica didn't care about her own reputation, but her mother did. Her mother also cared if Monica got hurt by her older but immature husband. Thus Jade's job was Owen's babysitter and PR shield when he did something with the potential for blowback on his wife and mother-in-law, which was disturbingly often.

Jade sent back a quick reply to her partner.

Owen shouldn't be too hard to find in this town. I'll take care of it alone and do damage control. I'll update you when I find something.

Relieved to have a task that had nothing to do with Carter's family, she sent off the message, checked her face one last time and left the bathroom.

She was carefully closing the bathroom door behind her, mind focused on the Van Tyle problem when she stumbled into a warm body and almost fell. A couple, older than her by at least twenty years, closed in on her to stop her from falling. Their hands fell away from each other and held her steady.

"Oh, excuse me!"

"It's fine, hon. Be careful, though, huh?" The woman of the couple flashed her a kind smile while the man steadied Jade on her feet.

Jade blushed. "Thank you."

Bright, attractive eyes, teak-brown skin and a familiar shape of jaw and chin told her the man was Carter's father. Which meant there was a high probability the woman was his mother. The man patted her shoulder and looped his arm around the woman's waist, his head dipping low to speak into her ear. A soft tittering laugh floated from the woman's lips and they disappeared down the hallway together, their hips bumping affectionately.

They looked to be in their midfifties, maybe in their sixties, but the affection between them made them seem like teenagers about to hook up. Jade blushed and, walking away from them, grabbed her phone and opened up a blank text message with Carter's name.

Jade: I'm lost in your house. How do I find my way out of the maze?

His reply came almost at once. Damn, he typed fast.

Carter: No need to go full CSI on me. I'm upstairs. Should I come down and get you?

Jade: No. Just tell me where you are. I'm upstairs too.

She followed his directions down the hallway, up another set of narrow stairs and into a small alcove. All the doors in the small wing were open. No Carter.

What the hell was this man up to? Jade crossed her arms over her chest and narrowed her gaze. The space was beautiful but sparsely occupied with most of the party happening downstairs on the first floor and outside. Up here, she heard the vague murmuring of conversation, but she felt like she was intruding. This space said home. It was no place she needed to be. She was an outsider. She didn't belong here.

At the end of the short hallway, a waist-high balcony shut off any possible progress forward. She leaned her hip against the balcony and pulled out her phone again.

"We need to go back and help Kingsley celebrate his fiancée," a low, feminine voice murmured from below her. It was the same voice that had warned her to be careful just moments before. Carter's mother.

"They won't miss us, at least not at this moment. Can you give me a few of these moments, hmm?" The man's voice was impossibly deep, and it reminded her of Carter's.

The woman laughed, a low and flirtatious trill of sound. Light footsteps sounded below Jade and she stepped back just as the pair came into view, still walking as closely together as when she saw them by the bathroom door. If anything, they were actually a little closer. The woman leaned her head onto the man's chest as they seemed to float together toward a long sofa tucked away in a picture window. The window overlooked a quiet garden blooming with flowers.

The man sat down first, and although there was plenty of room for two to sit side by side, the woman tucked herself into the man's lap and practically purred. He rumbled something to her Jade didn't hear and kissed her very intentionally on the lips. It was a kiss she returned with interest, in a show of passion that had Jade very nearly clutching her pearls. He tucked his chin close to her temple and pulled her even more into his lap.

"So what can I do for you, sir? What urgent matter do you have that is more important than wishing my son happy today?"

"Just the usual." He did something that made her squeal, probably a tickling Jade was too far away to see, and she laughed breathlessly but didn't try to get away. She only moved closer to him, wound her arms around his neck while her legs sprawled warmly over his lap.

They were beautiful together, and Jade wanted desperately to look away from them. But she couldn't. Her eyes would not move away from the older couple canoodling in the small alcove to temporarily escape the adoration of their children.

"You are a terrible man." The woman laughed breathlessly.

"What does that say about you? You're the one who married me."

Another soft giggle. "Very true…"

There was silence then, occasional sighs and the sound of kissing, bodies shifting in the cloth sofa. It was all too unspeakably intimate but Jade couldn't bring herself to move away and give them their privacy.

Never had she seen something like this before. They cared for each other. They wanted to be together and had sneaked away like teenagers to make out in a private— well, it would've been private if Jade hadn't been there— part of the house.

Her parents had never been like that with each other.

She'd only seen affection like that on television and, growing up with hypocrites who always said they were the perfect example of a family, Jade had wondered if that was the kind of marriage she'd end up with too.

Cold.

Bound by lies.

Loveless.

But in front of her was proof that it didn't have to be like that. Not even after thirteen children.

The thought jerked her upright and out of her morbid fascination with the older couple sharing a moment that should have been private.

God, she was so pathetic. Her unresolved feelings about her parents, about their deaths, were beginning to break down her defenses harder than she thought. Now they had her spying on people in their own house.

She cursed softly, turned and walked quietly away.

"I was wondering where you were." Carter appeared

out of nowhere, quiet on his size-eleven feet as if he were a much lighter man.

The stirred-up feelings in the pit of Jade's stomach roiled. Poisonous words bubbled up on the tip of her tongue.

"I was where you sent me," she muttered. "Which made me see things I wasn't ready for." She tipped her head toward the intimate alcove.

Carter lifted his gaze to where she pointed, and frowned. "Don't blame your stalking on me," he said. "I told you to meet me back there. Sure I got held up, but I didn't tell you to follow the oldies to whatever they're up to back there."

Whatever they're up to? Did this kind of thing happen often?

She nailed him with a narrow-eyed stare. "Are you trying to manipulate me or something?"

He scoffed at her. "It may be time for you to have a drink and relax." A dark brow rose as he looked back to where she'd come from, then he shook his head and a faintest touch of a smile curved his mouth. "Come on. I know where they hide the good stuff."

Jade let him lead her away. It was better than being a captive of her own imagination, thinking that she heard the couple kissing and laughing together again, happily ignoring the houseful of strangers and family roaming the place.

It wasn't long before she lost Carter again, though.

Someone else had a problem. Giving her an apologetic look, he asked her to stay by his side, but she shook her head and drifted off in a different direction while he went to play savior again.

Jade wandered.

The party, though so very obviously about family, was also focused on fun. Lots of different smells had teased her nose when she walked though the house. Fried ripe plantains. Rice and peas flavored with creamy coconut milk. Jerk chicken and jerk pork that she recognized from her year or so after college living next to a Jamaican restaurant that she visited *way* too often.

An outdoor grill sizzled with different types of shish kebabs and was being tended to by yet another guy in a waiter's uniform. Reggae music played through the house and the yard. The air of the party was festive and casual.

Only there for business, Jade felt out of place. Like she didn't belong. It was a familiar feeling, sticky and unpleasant that made her want to shelter herself in coldness and retreat again into a corner someplace to watch what she couldn't be a part of.

Jade fought the urge. No repeat visits to the middle school corner.

"I can tell you're wondering what you're doing here," Carter said.

Minus his suit jacket and with his sleeves rolled up, he sat down beside her on the bench where she'd been quietly enjoying the uncomplicated crowd and lush backyard.

Her parents' house didn't have anywhere near the amount of the space of this backyard but she bet it could have something similar. Flowers and maybe a gazebo, other things to complement the pool and modest size.

In San Diego, she had her little house, her tiny backyard on the mountainside, her circular pool and its Jacuzzi. But over the years, she'd come to accept that San Diego and all of California had become a sort of consolation prize for her.

Because of the complicated relationship with her parents, she'd written off the entire state of Florida. She'd wanted to go back for the warm ocean water, forever sun and Caribbean food. But could never bring herself to leave the safety of California after she'd gotten her business degree.

She'd been a coward then. She was a coward now.

Jade tore her eyes away from the beautiful yard. She'd always liked pretty things. Only recently had she been able to afford them and it felt nice.

"I am." She turned to Carter. "Your family is fantastic but they don't give me a sense at all of the company."

Kingsley was relaxed and casual, fun with his fiancée and the other members of his family. Nothing at all like he was at the office. Yes, Jade had met the wives but that meant nothing since none of them were involved in the family business.

"Maybe you haven't been paying attention to the right things," Carter said, his warm and deep voice rumbling over her. "You've been staring at the garden and just about everything else in this backyard all night instead of actually meeting the members of my family involved in the company."

Why was he paying such close attention to her?

And why was she letting that affect her so much?

"Was there something I missed?" she asked to get herself back on track.

"One or two," he said with that now familiar almost smile. "You want to come see?"

It wasn't like she was doing anything particularly interesting outside. "Sure." She fell in step beside him and took the arm he offered.

They walked toward the house and she couldn't help but notice the few heads that turned to watch them pass. Like before, it was nothing sinister, nothing hostile, just a look that said she was familiar to them somehow. Jade didn't understand when she'd never met any of them before.

"Your family is weird," she leaned over and said before she could think better of it. People were sensitive about their families, and she was sure Carter was no different. She internally winced, waiting for his reaction.

"They can be a little of that," he said with a subtle crinkling of the corners of his eyes.

Then she bit her lip, feeling guilty. Only a solid ten seconds chewing on her tongue kept her from apologizing. She wasn't comfortable here and that was no one's fault but her own. She didn't need to take it out on Carter or the family he so obviously loved and would do anything for.

As they walked through the yard and toward the house, a young boy around twelve peeled himself from a group of kids his own age. "Carter! Hold up." When Carter stopped, the boy held out his fist for a bump. "Thanks for taking care of the situation at school for me. Good looking out."

"You're welcome," Carter said, only slowing down enough to bump fists. "But you know you have to take care of it yourself next time, right?"

The boy mumbled and rolled his eyes. "I know." But there was no heat behind his words. If anything, only admiration for Carter who'd apparently done something for him that he was able but unwilling to do.

"Good. I'll see you at Lola's gallery opening later."

"For sure." The boy disappeared back into his group of friends.

Roughly the same thing happened four more times before they even made it to the back steps leading into the house.

It *was* a little amazing. "So, you are magic, huh?"

"Sometimes," he admitted with a negligent lift of a shoulder. "Sometimes not."

"When haven't you been?" she asked, genuinely curious.

"With you."

The comment shocked her for a moment and she could only blink in surprise while her body still moved on autopilot, putting one leg after the other, to stay at his side.

That was far from the truth.

But she didn't feel this was the place to tell him the extent of it. "Having you around has definitely changed my life."

"But not fixed anything you needed taking care of, though," he said, voice rumbling deep and sure.

All the things she'd gone through with him, because of him, because of her feelings for him back then and now. Although she'd wanted to blame him, he wasn't at fault in this. It took the two of them to make the decisions that had irrevocably changed her life ten years ago.

"Here we go." Carter pushed open the door to the living room.

It was nearly empty, with a pair of children playing jacks on the tiled floor and a couple tucked away in a corner love seat and having a laughing conversation complete with touches and playful shoves.

"Hey, Lola. Where are the parents?" Carter raised his voice.

The girl of the couple on the love seat tossed him a look over her shoulder. "Papa is upstairs having cigars with the boys. Mama, who knows?"

"Thanks." Carter threw the girl a wave that she raised her own hand to without looking back.

"It's upstairs we'll go, then," he said.

At Carter's side, Jade wound her way through the house. On their way through the mansion that was both showpiece and family warmth, he fended off more questions and requests for advice. He was graceful, calm, patient. And as she watched him answer question after question, his deep voice resonant and calm, she began to feel something that was both familiar and alien.

A warmth behind her breastbone. Prickling in her palms. The awareness of her heart picking up speed inside her chest.

Carter wasn't a handsome man to some. But to her, he was absolutely gorgeous. Breath-stealing. And he'd only gotten more devastatingly handsome over the years since they'd been apart. The bastard.

She wasn't exactly sure what had changed. But she tucked it away to look at more thoroughly later.

How did Carter put up with this all the time? The questions never stopped coming. Was this what it was like for him even as a kid in college?

At the bottom of the stairs as they were about to head up, Carter's phone rang.

He scowled briefly at the phone before he swiped across the screen to answer the call.

"Carter."

Jade made to move past him and continue up the stairs but he snagged a casual hand around her waist, a move that seemed both so unfamiliar and completely natural that she froze.

She turned in the strange embrace, inadvertently bringing herself even closer to him, her hip brushing against his, the scent of his aftershave rich in her nose. That feeling came over her again. A rush of awareness of him. Her body a sonar, pinging with his very nearness.

Move away.

She willed her legs to walk and leave him, but she couldn't move.

"I'll take care of it," he was saying to the person on the other line. He didn't seem happy about it. But did he seem happy overall? He was so completely cool, it was nearly impossible to tell.

She licked her lips, her heart thumping like a warning drum. She braced her palms against his chest and eased back, pushing against the warm and solid bulk of him. His voice vibrated beneath her palms, up her arms and into her own chest. A delicious shiver rocked through her.

He looked down at her, eyes warm and dark, but didn't let go.

Chill out, she told herself, staring up into his eyes. *Calm down. This is nothing. What you're feeling is just leftover stuff from before. It's* nothing.

"I'm a little busy now, but I'll deal with it tomorrow and let you know when it's done." He sounded like he was arranging a mob hit or something.

Jade rolled her eyes. She absolutely didn't want to know.

If nothing else, she had plausible deniability.

Her mind plucked different scenarios from the air of what he could be talking about. Anything to distract her from the feelings quivering through her body from his nearness.

"Good," he said, his voice tumbling down into its deeper registers. He was about to end the call. "Don't get into any more trouble in the meantime."

Trouble? Carter pulled the phone away from his ear and she grabbed his hand.

"What kind of trouble are you getting into?"

"Trouble? Me? Never, Ms. Tremaine. When have you known me to ever step in something I wasn't sure of?" His eyes gleamed down at her. "Can you say the same thing about yourself?"

The sound of footsteps from above them on the stairs yanked her gaze from Carter. Jade blinked.

A sleek, young body in a catsuit. A beautiful and familiar face full of mischief. The girl galloped down the steps wearing a huge smile, her hair flying around her face like a dark, wild and living thing. She looked just as wild and happy as the last time Jade had seen her.

"I'm so glad you could come." Giggling, Dee threw her arms around Jade and squeezed.

Chapter 7

Jade jerked out of her shock at seeing Dee the last place she expected. "What are you doing here?"

"Because I live here, silly." Dee drew back from their hug. "At least I do sometimes. I have my own place, but I kinda like my folks, so I'm here a lot."

Jade felt like she was living in the twilight zone. Or at least like she was looking at Dee with her mouth hanging open. "Your folks?"

"Yes. Carter here is my beloved brother, and I would do just about anything for him." And she looked at the big guy with a smile and something else Jade could not identify. "Jaxon, though, can go play in traffic. Twins or not, he is a pain in my whole entire ass." Dee squeezed Carter's arm and turned back to Jade. "By the way, did you have fun with him at the club? Don't tell me I wasted my time setting that up."

The club? Of course. No wonder she couldn't find Dee once she and Carter had run into each other. God damn…

Jade didn't like to think of herself as dumb, but this whole situation was just weird. It stank of blatant manipulation, something she'd just stupidly accused Carter of. As if he knew all her triggers and the emotional black hole she lived in.

"So you didn't think it was important to tell me that you are a Diallo, that Jaxon Diallo is your brother. That Kingsley is your brother?"

Dee's pretty face frowned up. "It was important to you but not to me." She shook her head and wrinkled her nose.

Jade couldn't help it. She stared at Dee as if the girl had lost her ever-loving mind. What was up with these Diallos anyway?

So far Kingsley was the only one who hadn't rubbed her the wrong way. Or who hadn't gone out of his way to make her want to give them throat chop, chop to the throat.

As if he had read her mind, Carter leaned close to Jade. "We're not all bad, I promise. Paxton is just a little special. All the geniuses in the family are."

He lightly pushed Paxton away with the fond smile. "Ease up, girl. I can see exactly what you're doing."

"It's not like I'm trying to hide it." Paxton gave her brother an impish grin and Jade looked from one Diallo to the other wondering what she was missing.

"I don't need your help," Carter rumbled, and the sound was almost defensive.

"I beg to differ, brother dear." Paxton giggled and

tossed her black, dandelion hair. "In this instance, you definitely need all the help I can give you."

She had never been one to shy away from questions. Either asking or answering them.

The young girl was as pretty as the last time Jade saw her. Vibrant and mischievous. But something different sparkled in her whiskey-brown eyes. A different set of worries, maybe. Like something had been settled for her recently that had worried her before.

"What's going on here?"

"Nothing that Carter won't tell you about later." She dimpled again at Jade then lightly punched Carter in the arm. "Welcome to our home, Jade. If I don't bump into you again later, I'm sure I'll be seeing you again soon." She jumped to her tiptoes and kissed Carter's cheek, then she was off, slipping through the endlessly moving group of beautiful people in the Diallo house.

"Well, that wasn't weird at all." Jade tipped a look over her shoulder then turned fully to face Carter. "Do members of your family often go by aliases out in the world?"

"Aliases?"

"Yes. I met your sister before but she introduced herself as Dee, not Paxton."

He gave a long-suffering sigh. "Somehow I'm not surprised. That girl goes her own way most times. Even when it looks like the path to destruction."

"I can see that."

"Don't worry about it too much, though." His hand drifted from her shoulder and down her back. "You'll only end up in the nuthouse yourself trying to make sense of them. Of us." Amusement made his eyes gleam, but otherwise it didn't look like he was joking.

"How did I get involved with you guys?" she said, shaking her head. Why hadn't she known that Carter came from a big and crazy-making family before now?

"You were overwhelmed by my amazing charm and irresistible sexiness?" An eyebrow rose. The sleek rise of the dark, manicured brow only showed off the un-smiling but devastatingly sexy shape of his mouth.

Jade's heart skipped with sudden panic. She couldn't be falling for him all over again. She couldn't.

Run. Run. Run.

She cleared her throat. "It's time for me to head out. Any business I have is pretty much over."

"Are you sure?" The shape of Carter's hand burned into the small of her back.

"Positive." Her heart beat so loudly, she could barely hear herself talk. "I think it's time I got out of your hair and let you enjoy your family in peace."

A line of worry settled between Carter's eyes. "Let me drive you back to your hotel, then."

"No, I can just cab it from here."

"Absolutely not. I'm not going to abandon you, Jade."

She opened her mouth to protest again.

"Don't make an asshole out of me, Jade."

A sigh leaked from her lips. She'd be the asshole, though, if she took him away from his family and this celebration of his brother's happiness. Even she wasn't clueless enough to let that happen. She took a step back and gritted her teeth against the flood of disappointment when his hand fell away from her skin.

What was *wrong* with her?

"Okay. Fine." The devil made her reach out and brace her palms against his chest—he was so warm!—and lift her face to his intent gaze. "I'll stay as long as you're here."

Doubt clouded his compelling features.

Jade bit her lip. Her fingers curled themselves into the soft fabric of his suit. "I promise."

When she said the words, his gaze cleared. "Good." He stepped closer and then, against her better judgment, became connected by her touch and his. His hands settled on her hips, burning in her even more thoroughly than that first touch. "Now, come, let me introduce you around to the rest of the family. They'll want to know who's going to save our bacon despite Jaxon's foolishness."

She bowed to the inevitable, maybe not gracefully, but with certainty. "Okay. That works. But I'll need more of that rum punch. I swear you guys put something in it."

"Never." But his faint smile was pure mischief, and when she got her refill she sniffed it a few times to see if it had anything crazy in it. But all she smelled was her own self-delusion.

After a couple of hours, she managed to meet every member of the family, including Dee again, whose name was apparently Paxton.

They all looked her over as if they knew her and because of that, their smiles and hugs of welcome frightened her just a little. But despite herself, she ended up having a bit of a good time. Even chatted with Carter's parents, his mother who she knew was COO but didn't know what a woman with a steel spine looked like until the person she'd caught cuddled with her husband in a hidden alcove also proved to be absolutely unbendable, graceful and a little frightening.

"So, you're the one," Carter's mother said to Jade after the toasts had been made to Kingsley and Adah.

"The one?" She stared back at the beautiful older woman. "Oh, you mean the one who Kingsley hired to help with the…situation? Yes," she plowed ahead before his mother could answer. What else could she be asking about?

"Of course, dear. What else could I be talking about?" Hyacinth Diallo looked past Jade's shoulder at someone or something, but Jade kept it cool and managed not to turn around and look in that direction. "You seem like a lovely woman, my dear. I hope you'll be able to fit in to the position as well as my children think."

Fit in to the position? But she had already been hired. It was a done deal. But again, she didn't ask for any clarification. That was what Carter was there for.

When most of the people had already flowed out the door and on to another event much more interesting than what Jade was heading to after this, Carter found her at the punch bowl chatting with Lola Diallo about California and the merits of San Diego over Miami.

The woman knew a lot of San Diego and seemed to like it well enough, although at the end of their conversation, Jade actually thought she hated it a little and had the opinion that anyone wanting happiness needed to move immediately to Miami.

But Jade hadn't known much happiness in Miami. Only in theory when she'd had stupid, and brief, thoughts of moving back there with a family of her own.

"Miami has its downside," Lola said with a careful shrug of her narrow and elegant shoulders. "But have you checked out all the cool stuff to do here? The place has changed a little bit since you were a naive college kid."

"It hasn't changed that much," Jade said. From what she saw, except for a few buildings, smaller bikinis and higher taxes, things had stayed pretty much the same. And that same place was not somewhere she would ever consider living.

"You ready, Jade?" Carter appeared at her shoulder, tucking his phone in his pocket.

The man lived with that damn phone in his hand. With all his responsibilities, it only made sense, though.

"Sure," she said. "Whenever you are."

The siblings exchanged a look and Carter's jaw flexed. "In that case, let's go. I'll take you back to your hotel before it gets too much later."

It was already nudging close to midnight. The daytime engagement party had turned into a nighttime celebration, complete with dancing in the gazebo and pretty much anywhere in the house there was room to move.

"Okay." Jade smiled in apology at Lola. "It was great to meet you. Maybe we'll see each other again soon." And she wasn't lying. She'd liked talking with the extroverted and slightly irreverent woman who was nothing like Carter.

"I'm sure we will," Lola said. Then leaned in to squeeze Jade in a tight hug. "Don't let this one drive you off. We like having you around and would love for you to come back around more often."

We?

But before she could think to ask, Lola was nudging Carter's shoulder and walking off toward the kitchen to scandalize someone else.

It didn't take long for her and Carter to say their goodbyes and climb back into his gorgeous car.

They drove for miles before Jade thought of anything to say. The whole day had been a bit surreal.

"Your family seems nice."

"You'll realize the error of that statement soon enough," he said drily. "They do like you though, which is why they were on their best behavior."

Jade choked on an unexpected breath of laughter. *Best* behavior?

Thinking of the steady stream of dirty jokes Lola told her all night and the identity trick Paxton played on her, she wondered briefly how the family treated people it *didn't* like.

The smile fell from her face but the warmth from Carter, from the evening with his beautiful family, remained.

"Jade."

She lifted her head to look at Carter as the car slowed to a stop at a light. His dark eyes settled on her, heavy and warm.

"I didn't say it before, but I want to tell you now." His deep voice sent ripples of awareness into her belly.

"Thank you for staying with me and my family tonight. It means a lot."

"I—" *I didn't know how much I wanted to stay until you asked me.* "You're welcome. It wasn't so bad."

But she made sure he saw the humor in her eyes. Carter huffed a laugh and turned his attention back to the road.

More miles passed.

Jade breathed into the strangely comfortable silence and curled into the luxurious leather seat. The sensuous leather smell and movement of the cityscape past her window accompanied her confused thoughts for the rest of the ride.

Beside her, Carter handled the car with sensual speed and efficiency, hand always on the gearshift, his eyes straight ahead except for the few times he glanced briefly her way. The definition of quiet strength.

He was a good man. Not at all the runner she labeled him as after he disappeared on her in college. So now, where did that leave her and the anger she'd carried around against him for so long?

In its own way, that anger had been comforting. It was familiar.

Now, though, she had to put it aside.

But what else did she have to hold on to?

Chapter 8

"So are you absolutely sure you don't want to keep the property?"

Jade, pretending to be relaxed in the chair across from the lawyer's desk, curled her toes in the royal blue stilettos she'd worn on a whim. Well, not quite on a whim. After seeing Carter and being battered by her own uncertain feelings, she'd needed every confidence booster possible. So she'd put on one of the sexiest dresses in her suitcase, screw-me-silly shoes, done her makeup to savage perfection and shown up again at the lawyer's office.

Of course, she rationalized it by saying she had a later dinner with her cousin after this—a cousin she'd only known as a kid wanted to give her condolences in person on her parents' death. She'd told Melody it was no problem, no condolences needed, but her cousin had been insistent and Jade hadn't had enough willpower to push back and claim an evening eating ice cream and watching reality TV for herself.

So, yes. Here she was at her lawyer's office, or her parents' lawyer's office, dressed to kill—or at least for sex—while he tried to convince her she didn't hate the idea of keeping the house where her childhood died.

"I intend to sell it." She turned her wrist to look at her watch. "I've already signed the papers necessary for claiming their estate." A fancy term for what was basically their house, the furniture in it, her mother's little Honda Civic and the few dollars they'd saved up over the years. None of which Jade needed.

Even with the job of dealing with the Diallo's problem child—or at least the one who was giving them problems at the moment—all she wanted to do was jump on the fastest plane out of Miami and get back to her normal and Carter-free life in San Diego.

There, she wouldn't have to worry about the annoying pulses of feeling for Carter that pressed under her skin whenever she was near him. Or thought of him. Or when he was in Miami with her.

God...

"Did you say something?" The lawyer looked at her with obviously faked concern.

"Nothing you're listening to, apparently." She stopped swinging her foot. "Listen. Just do as I ask." She might just be done playing nice. "This...flotsam is nothing I want or need. Let's just arrange for the sale of the lot. I'll sign whatever you need to make that happen."

Another frown of concern. "Ms. Tremaine—"

And then she'd had enough. "I have another appointment, Mr. Harris. If you can't handle my parents' affairs as I've instructed, then I'll have someone else tend to it."

The man's mouth tightened. "No. We are perfectly capable of dealing with the estate as you've requested. It just seems a shame—"

"Perfect." Jade got to her feet. "That's all I need. Please start the process." With a flick of her fingers, she adjusted the drape of the dress over her legs then shouldered her purse. "Thank you for your time with this and, of course, your promptness in dealing with this matter."

A sputter of words left his mouth as he stood up so she wouldn't loom over him. "If you're sure…"

"I am." She offered him her hand to shake over the desk then turned to leave as soon as that basic courtesy was exchanged. "Have a good day, Mr. Harris. And thank you so much for your time."

With the harsh thud of her heart in her ears, she practically ran out of the office, down the short flight of stairs and into the early evening. The lukewarm Miami air rushed into her lungs.

In. Out. And again.

Even from the grave, it seemed like her parents were intent on torturing her. Cold fingers clutched at the strap of her purse, but she held her head up and marched to the cool and elegant lines of her car in the parking lot where it was by no means the only expensive ride.

She badly needed to blow away the agitation the conversation with the lawyer had stirred back up. A drive with the windows down and her music blasting loud enough to obliterate her thoughts was just the trick.

* * *

An hour later found her at the restaurant where her cousin wanted to meet.

The bright October full moon and cool Miami city lights surrounded her when she climbed out of her car and began making her way toward the sidewalk seating where her cousin told her she would be waiting.

The sidewalk area overflowed with a laughing and drinking crowd, a typical Miami sight Jade had never been part of in her hometown. Home. Parents. Homework. Fears of what she was missing while her peers had whole "sinful" lives.

A quick glance at her watch told her she was at least fifteen minutes early and she headed toward the front door of the restaurant.

"Jade!"

Startled, she stopped at the sound of her name. A woman in gray stood up from a table for two, waving. "Hey, cuzzo!"

Cuzzo?

She threw out a smile and detoured to the woman who, as she drew closer, coalesced into the familiar features of one of the kids, her aunt's only girl, she used to play with as a child.

Jade's footsteps faltered as fragments of memories came back to her.

Running around a cluttered backyard.

Eating peanut-butter-and-jelly sandwiches with two other children at a kitchen table while music played and a woman, plump and flashing a gold tooth, sang along.

Swapping stories from the bottom of a bunk bed.

Yes, she had played with other children when she

was younger. She'd always been isolated in her parents' lake view house and away from "outside" influences.

But it wasn't long before her father put the brakes on those playdates with his sister's children, insisting that Jade being with her cousins would lead to a life of looseness and sin. Never mind that she hadn't even been eleven years old yet when they were yanked out of her life.

"Hi, Melody."

She was vaguely aware of eyes on her as she made her way to her cousin, her hips swinging in the high heels and soft A-line dress.

Now that Jade wasn't elbows deep in worry about her parents or property or anything else, she remembered how Melody's parents had been nightclub singers and musicians. They'd loved to sing at gatherings. And Melody actually had a great singing voice. But she still didn't know why her cousin had reached out to her.

"You got a hot date tonight, girl?" Melody asked with a teasing smile.

She was gorgeous and deliciously thick with her wide hips, generous bosom, and wide mouth showing off a warm and giving smile. Her wavy, permed hair was thick and long around her face and shoulders, and she wore a gray dress and purple shoes and looked ready for a photo shoot.

The memories came rushing back and they made her smile. Her cousin, irreverent and with a smart mouth at eleven. A talented singer who could read music and had already memorized over a dozen songs and had written one of her own by the time she and Jade had been ripped from each other's lives.

"Do *you* have a hot date?"

Melody sucked her teeth and gave Jade a playful sideways look. "Girl, I stay ready for Mr. Right in these competitive streets!"

Jade couldn't help it. She laughed long and loud as she and Melody exchanged a lasting and warm hug.

"Well, obviously you look great," Jade said as she sat down.

"Thanks, girl. You're not too bad," Melody said. The look she gave Jade's dress, shoes and hair said that was a hell of an understatement.

Only two glasses of water and a place setting for two sat on the small table.

"Thanks." She flashed her cousin a smile, suddenly glad that she came. "You look amazing. I love those shoes."

Melody's eyes twinkled. "Wanna exchange?" She knew good and damn well the difference in the prices of the shoes was as far as the earth was from the moon.

"I'll let you know after a glass or two of wine."

"In that case, let's get to it!" Melody signaled a passing waiter.

They settled down to a shared bottle of midpriced but delicious dessert wine—Jade wasn't very hungry and Melody confessed to a large and late lunch before she got to the restaurant.

"Thanks for coming out to meet me, Jade. I know you weren't feeling it."

Jade shrugged, not bothering to lie. They hadn't seen each other since they were children, true, but even at the peril of hurting someone's feelings, Jade wasn't in the habit of lying to family.

"Your call caught me by surprise," she said instead.

"I bet." Melody winked at her, honest to God winked. "But when I heard about your parents, I figured you'd come this way. Since I didn't have your number, I asked the lawyer to pass your info my way and here we are."

"Here we are," Jade repeated. She sipped from her long-stemmed glass and rolled the sweet red over her tongue.

Melody's game was warm and fond, even a little nostalgic. "I'm sorry we weren't able to keep in touch. My folks didn't want me to piss your father off."

Understandable. For a spiritual man, her father had a hell of a temper.

"Held a lot of people by a short leash," she said. In school, he and her mother determined what friends she had, what her school activities were, what she knew about the world. And she had been too scared to push back against any of it.

Only when she'd escaped to college and ended up meeting Carter had she made her very first decisions about more than basic things as an adult.

And her father had been the very first one to throw the consequences of that right in her face.

"But you're okay now, right?" A frown of concern sat between Melody's bright eyes. Artificially lightened to a strange gray, they matched her dress.

"More or less." Jade let her shrug speak for her.

"I'm sorry, honey." The pity in her cousin's face twisted like a knife in Jade's stomach.

"Nothing to be sorry for. None of it was your fault. We were both kids, right?"

"Yeah, but I could have at least…I don't know. Asked my parents to help you out?" She looked as helpless sitting across the table as she must have felt as a child.

"They had kids and a life and worries of their own. Please, it's fine, Mel. Really." The old nickname fell naturally off her tongue and her cousin smiled softly at the sound of it. "The present is what counts."

"Well, in that case, tell me what you're doing now, in the present."

Jade shrugged again. "Working. Dealing with the house they left me. I'm selling it as soon as possible and taking my butt back to California."

"Oh…" Melody paused with her wineglass held up to her lips. "You're not sticking around?"

"I don't—" The trill of Jade's cell phone, a tone that belonged to her office in San Diego, interrupted her. "Oh, sorry. I have to take this." She fished the phone out of her bag. "Hey, Corrie."

"Hopefully I'm not interrupting anything important," her partner greeted her, sounding irritated and distracted. The clicking of computer keys came clearly through the phone.

"You are, but you're already on the phone so lay it on me."

"Van Tyle is up to some real obvious foolishness right now. In your town. Not far from you, in fact."

"Seriously…?"

"If I had any sort of sense of humor left, I sure wouldn't be using it right now," Corrie muttered.

"Okay, I'll go handle it."

"Are you sure?"

Jade barely restrained herself from rolling her eyes at Corrie. "That's what you called for me to do, right?"

"I was just trying to be polite and respectful of whatever thing you have going on now."

This time, Jade did roll her eyes. "Thanks. But you know as well as I do that business is never secure enough for us to blow off a client and not expect repercussions."

The day before, when Corrie had sent the message to Jade about Owen Van Tyle, Jade didn't doubt she could deal with it.

While at the engagement party, she'd put out a few feelers for the errant husband but nothing panned out beyond a confirmation that he was in Miami and spending an alarming amount of cash. The search during that day before her visit to the lawyer had yielded practically the same thing.

Still being optimistic, she had the firm plant some dummy tracks on social media via Instagram and Twitter about him partying but waiting with amorous impatience for his wife to get back from a conference in Canada. But according to the follow-up pic Corrie sent, waiting for his wife wasn't exactly what Owen Van Tyle was up to.

"Okay," Jade said again, this time with a sigh in her voice.

She really didn't want to leave Melody. They'd been actually having a real conversation about things that mattered. Things Jade had forgotten.

It was just plain *nice* to sit with someone she considered family and who didn't use that label as yet another way to hurt her. "No worries, Corrie. I'll go reel him in."

She hung up the phone.

"Gotta go?" Melody asked around another sip of her wine.

"Yes. I'm sorry." The disappointment rang loud and clear in her voice. "But I want us to do this again. Or at least to do it better next time."

"You're on call like a doctor or something, huh?" her cousin asked while Jade pulled thirty dollars from her wallet.

"It's nothing that meaningful, believe me. People basically pay me a lot of money to babysit other people and tell lies in public forums."

"The pay must be pretty good." A hint of a tease sparkled in Melody's eyes.

"I can't complain." Jade stood up. "I'll buzz you tonight, okay. I…" She pursed her lips and wondered just how honest she should be. Then she shrugged. What the hell? There wasn't much else for her to lose. "To be honest, I didn't really want to come meet you. But I'm glad I did. Something happened a couple of days ago that made me realize how important family is."

Melody's face lost some of its joyful carelessness, leaving a soft smile in its place. "Yeah… I'm glad. And it's really cool that you came out even though you had doubts. That means your dad didn't squeeze all the family-love out of you."

Jade aimed for a smile but instead felt her lips curl down a little in sadness. Sometimes she did think all the "family-love" in her was gone. Her parents had spent so many years isolating her from her relatives until Jade felt she had no one in the world but them. And then her parents were gone too, leaving her completely alone.

Warmth glowed in Jade's chest. Maybe she didn't have to be alone after all.

Swiftly, she leaned down and hugged Melody. "See you soon, Mel."

Then she left the restaurant feeling lighter than when she'd come in.

Chapter 9

Kingsley's fiancée was going to kill him. And she might even enjoy every moment of it.

Carter curled up his mouth around the faintly bad taste in it. One of Leo's cheap cigars. "This is the worst idea you've ever had, Leo."

"You're just jealous you didn't think of it first." Leo knocked back another shot of tequila and watched the show unfold in front of them with far too much pride.

A strangled sound left Carter's throat and he brought the glass of seltzer water to his mouth to help get rid of the taste of cigars from his tongue. The so-called sexy lighting in the VIP lounge, low and in shades of red and purple, swirled around his brother's laughing face. Leo looked like mischief on a particularly wicked day.

The Kingsley before he'd met and fallen in love with Adah had been a dog. Just a few notches on the bedpost shy of a man whore. Back in the day—basically last year—he had a trailer load of women parading in and out of his bedroom. But the man who came back from Aruba didn't see any other women. For Kingsley, Adah was the only woman of his heart, of his bed. Period.

Then he allowed Leo to arrange a bachelor party for him. Maybe he should've told Leo Adah was the only woman for his lap too.

Leo was one of the last remaining single brothers, owned a string of successful nightclubs in the city, so it made sense at the time. At least to everyone but Carter. Leo had the devil's own sense of humor and usually got away with half the stuff he did because he was charming and had the killer Diallo smile. Carter had tried to warn Kingsley not to ask Leo to plan anything. But away from business, no one paid Carter and his warnings any mind. Which was why they were now doing way too much at one of the most exclusive strip clubs in Miami, i.e. watching an Adah look-alike give Kingsley a lap dance.

His brothers, their male friends and Leo's twin, Lola, who'd insisted on coming to the club with them laughed and encouraged the whole thing.

"I hope this doesn't come back to bite you all in the ass," Carter rumbled.

"Come on, who's going to tell Adah?"

That wasn't one of Leo's smartest questions. Adah, even more than any other woman who married into the family, had been completely embraced by everyone. By the other wives of course, but especially by the girls in the family who'd always felt outnumbered by the nine brothers who ran around high on testosterone most of the time.

Usually, his brothers used their power for good. Leo, though…

Carter mentally shrugged. This wasn't his problem anyway. He was here for the fun, but as usual, part of him was on the lookout for any way this could turn bad, so he could fix it. Sipping his tonic water, he hoped there would be no need for his "magic" tonight, but with his brothers, all he could do was hope.

"Come on, honey. You sure you can't do that?" Carter's ear picked up the wheedling voice under the cover of the loud, sensual music the girls danced to.

The VIP lounge was big. Massive, actually. Away from the main part of the club, the high rollers could safely and easily indulge in as many lap dances and private conversations as they could pay for. But they had to do it in a shared room with other big-money customers.

Only floor-to-ceiling velvet curtains—thick and deep purple—separated Kingsley's bachelor party from the other groups in the large room. Somehow, the club had rigged it so the music from each enclosed area—roughly a hundred square feet—didn't leak to any of the others. But if you weren't hearing impaired, you could just about hear every word between the dancers and the people who paid for their attention.

Carter determinedly sipped his glorified water and turned his ear away from what was clearly not his business. Unlike most places where cash could just about buy you anything, this club strongly discouraged sex between the girls and the clients. Not just big and sturdy-looking guys at the doors and hovering nearby, but it had cameras in all the cordoned-off areas too. If they saw something foolish going down, they'd swoop in and take care of it. In theory anyway.

So he ignored the guy throwing money around and trying to get the dancer to use her mouth for more than talking.

In their area, he had enough to worry about with a slightly tipsy Kingsley being set up by their mischievous younger brother.

"Fiancée or no, I would've made a play for that dancer a long time ago," Leo said to Carter.

"That's because you don't have a woman you like for more than a couple of weeks at a time and want to keep."

Leo looked at him with mockery in his eyes. "You talk like *you* have a woman like that."

Carter sipped his water and ignored him in favor of turning his sympathetic gaze back to his oldest brother.

Kingsley sat in the chair of honor in the center of the room, a couple of his shirt buttons undone, his sleeves rolled up to his elbows. The woman rolled her gorgeous body all over Kingsley's lap. Smiling with her plush and damp burgundy lips, she grabbed his hands and brought them to her waist. Each time, he pulled his hands back and put them on his own thighs. He stayed smiling, a lazy tilt of his lips that with Kingsley could mean anything.

He wasn't feeling her up, but he wasn't pushing her away either. Then again, Kingsley was never one to burst anyone's bubble. Leo and Kingsley's best friend, Victor, wanted to throw him a bachelor party he wouldn't forget. This was certainly it.

Starting at ten in the morning, it had been an all-day celebration. A lavish breakfast catered by Victor. Postbreakfast drinks on a boat sailing Biscayne Bay. Parasailing over the brilliant blue water, more food, more drinks, smack-talking and, finally, the strip club.

On the day before the wedding, Carter assumed Adah was having an equally debauched good time with her matron of honor and bridesmaids. Maybe even with male strippers. But it probably didn't include strippers. Probably. Like the rest of the family, Carter already loved Adah, but he didn't know her that well.

"This thing isn't gonna take care of itself, honey." The coaxing voice from behind the velvet curtain on the other side of the vast room made Carter twitch.

Where the hell were the guys who were supposed to be keeping these girls from being harassed?

A movement nearby caught his eye, and Victor, just about the only other guy who wasn't eyeballing the stripper or fending off the attentions of the other two girls Leo paid to be in the room, stood up with his jaw clenched and his eyes narrowed at the cordoned-off area where the voice was coming from.

So, Carter wasn't the only one concerned.

Good. Sometimes Carter worried he was hyper-aware of things around him. Too concerned about what was going on in the lives around him to pay attention to his own.

He stood up and joined Victor. After exchanging a look, the two of them swept aside their own heavy curtain and headed into the main part of the room.

Just then, the door banged open and stopped them in their tracks.

The noise wasn't a loud one, but it was enough to draw Carter's attention.

A woman stalked into the room. Two men big enough to put Carter's height and muscles to shame walked in alongside her like the hulking wings of an otherwise gorgeous and delicate bird.

Jade?

Yes. Jade.

A current of electricity ran down Carter's spine and settled like a warm hand in his lap. Since the engagement party, thoughts of her came as easily and frequently as his next breath. The dream that wouldn't leave him alone for over ten years suddenly disappeared. Instead, he woke every morning aching. The touch of his own hand never satisfied him, so he didn't even try.

And now, here she was.

"Give me a sec," he muttered to Victor then signaled a passing waitress for a whiskey.

"You all right, man?" Victor looked at him like he worried for Carter's sanity.

Oh, yeah. Of course. He never drank when he was on the clock. And over the years, his default behavior was to act as if he was working. Even when he was with his family. And *everyone* knew that.

"Yeah, I'm good." He gulped the whiskey as soon as the waitress brought it over.

In the meantime, Jade and her mammoth wings swept around the large room. They took the long way, somehow avoiding the plush lounge where Kingsley was putting his future married life in danger.

Somehow, Carter wasn't surprised when she pushed aside the curtain shielding the section where the concerning sounds were coming from.

"Good. I'm glad someone is going to handle that asshole." Lola sauntered up, sipping on something pink and frothy. "I was just about to complain about him to somebody."

Unlikely.

Carter thought her more likely reaction would've been to stomp over there and drag the guy off the stripper. Lola, half of a set of twins with more courage than common sense, did not take crap from anybody. And sometimes got into trouble only her much bigger brothers could get her out of.

"What's that woman going to do, anyway?" Lola craned her head to see what was going on in the other VIP section. "It's not like she works here or owns the place."

She didn't, but Carter didn't wonder what she was doing at the strip club. Getting to know this version of Jade—capable, successful, busy—was like meeting a whole new woman. And as a PR pro, he saw for himself how very hands-on she was. The girl he knew before wasn't the type to burst into a strip club with obvious muscle by her side. But, more and more every day, he was coming to realize that this Jade Tremaine wasn't the woman, or girl, he knew all those years ago.

The sounds from the other VIP section changed. The voice of the high roller from before growling low with aggression. Jade's response, though indistinguishable, was steady and calm. Even when High Roller let loose a few curse words.

"You can't treat me like this! I'm Owen Van Tyle!"

Whatever that meant, it apparently didn't mean very much to Jade because moments later she walked out, behind the tall men this time. They firmly held a young and moderately attractive guy between them. High Roller, Carter assumed.

The two big guys firmly marched the self-proclaimed Owen Van Tyle out of the curtained-off room and toward the main door of the VIP area. Jade followed them, whipping out her phone as she walked, without once looking for a second in Carter's direction. Her high heels stabbed the floor with each step.

Seconds later, the curtains of Van Tyle's VIP area flapped open and a relieved-looking dancer ran out. Followed by another dancer, then yet another.

How many women did that guy have in there with him anyway?

"Isn't that Jade? Your...whatever?" Lola pinned Carter with a questioning look.

"Yeah!" Leo popped up out of nowhere. "At first, I was thinking the girls here just got hotter—" Carter growled at him but Leo just grinned and kept going "—then I got a better look." Leo waggled his eyebrows. "So, are you going to finally make your move or what?"

"You can stop right there," Carter muttered. But he couldn't take his eyes off the door Jade had disappeared through. Even now, the remembered sway of her hips was making his pants feel just a little bit too tight.

Lola pressed her smiling lips together and shot Leo

a look. "You know Carter doesn't like it when you tease him."

"Yeah, is that why you do it so much?"

The two of them laughed. At Carter.

Through the slightly parted velvet drapes, Carter saw that Kingsley and the dancer were still doing... whatever it was that lap dancing consisted of and weren't paying them any attention. Same for everyone else in their area. The other men chatted up strippers and cheered on Kingsley, building up a ruckus it was damn near impossible to hear anything over.

That was all fine by Carter. He stared again at the door Jade had disappeared through.

He turned to Leo. "I'm going to see what's going on."

"Good boy." Leo laughed. "You'll learn to take care of your own wants and desires yet, brother." He clapped Carter on the shoulder and headed back to the action.

"What does he mean by that?" Carter frowned.

Lola went up on her tiptoes and landed a kiss on his cheek, and Carter automatically looped a hand around her small waist to briefly hold her close. "You'll figure it out." Then she was gone too.

Why were his sisters always telling him that?

He thought he managed to wait an admirably long time—just enough to prove he had *some* self-control— before rushing out the door after her. Carter found Jade just inside the back door of the strip club, wishing the bouncer a nice night. Carter slowed down to enjoy the sight of her, figure on sleek display in the clinging red dress, the super-high heels that made her legs look even more amazing. The rocking curve of her hips and butt as she walked away from him nearly made him moan out loud.

Damn. She'd gotten even more beautiful, no, sexier, over the years. And the last time they'd been together— at his parents' house—her dress had been elegant and restrained, the perfect compromise between business and family-friendly. But this red dress. Sweet baby Jesus… It clung to her body and moved against her sensual curves in a way that seemed deliberately designed to make him crazy. She wasn't a stripper but from her brief walk through the packed club, he'd noticed nearly every pair of eyes in the place followed her, obviously mentally stripping her naked and putting her up there on the pole with the other girls.

But her look was beyond stripper sexy. She was elegant and mouthwatering and every step she took made him want to drop to his knees in worship of her stunning body and the tartness inevitably waiting for him on her lips.

Okay. Control yourself, man!

In the hour or so he'd been in the club with his brothers, none of the women had affected him like this. Not a single one.

Shifting himself where he stood, Carter cleared his throat and kept walking despite the sudden rock-hard obstacle in his pants.

Ahead of him, Jade had her phone in her hand and an intent look on her face. When she slipped out the door, he followed. Inside the jacket of his sports coat, his phone rang, but he ignored it.

Her eyes roved around the secluded parking lot like

she was expecting someone or something to hop out of the bushes. Paparazzi?

She stood next to the open driver's side passenger door of a black town car. With her arms crossed over her chest, cell phone held easily in one hand, she said something to the person in the car. Through the open passenger door, he could see the high roller in the back, firmly trapped between the two hulking guys. From the guy's curses, he wasn't too happy with how his party ended.

"I already let his wife know everything is under control," Jade said. "Just get him back to the hotel. She'll meet him there in less than an hour."

A low-voiced response came from inside the car. One of the big guys, Carter assumed.

"Yes," Jade said. "He'll calm down once the liquor wears off but keep an eye on him anyway. We don't want this to spin out of control."

Another inaudible reply came and she nodded. The passenger door of the limo closed and she stepped back to allow the sleek black vehicle to pull away from the curb.

"Jade!"

She looked over her shoulder with a distracted smile when he called her name.

"Hey, Carter."

"What are you doing here?" he asked, although from the conversation he'd just overheard, it was fairly obvious. But she tended to burn the common sense out of his brain.

"Work," she simply said. "What about you?" Then

she looked up at the marquee of the club with a wry glance. "I didn't figure this for your type of place."

"Why, you think I don't do strip clubs?"

"Not at all. I'm sure you're a man with all the usual needs." Her lips pursed. "This place seems a bit too... obvious for someone like you."

He moved closer to her on the sidewalk, hands in his pockets. Mr. Casual. "You said it before—there are a lot of things we don't know about each other anymore."

"You're very right." She nodded, looking thoughtful. Then sighed and ran a hand over her short hair. "Anyway, I'll leave you to it. I'm sure the girls are anxious for you to get back in there."

"They're doing just fine," he said with a dismissive shrug. The dancers were nothing for him to worry about. "I'm here with my brothers for Kingsley's bachelor party. As long as he's there, the party will keep going."

"Ah..." Another of her smiles curved that lush mouth he hadn't been able to get out of his mind for ten years. "See you around, then."

Jade tucked her phone away in her purse and headed toward the silver car parked all the way on the other side of the full parking lot.

She was leaving. Just like she had a few days before. Just like *he* had ten years ago. It seemed like they were always walking away from each other, no matter who did it first.

And the first time, just like now, he had walked away from her because of something he thought the family needed from him. Back then, the situation had been dire. He had to leave. But he hadn't spared even a moment to tell her what was going on and let her know that he wanted to continue the thing they'd started. That was his fault. But that was also in the past.

For right now, he couldn't let them keep walking away from each other.

"Dinner," he said, walking faster to catch up with her. "Have dinner with me tonight."

She turned around, walking slowly backward, quite a feat on heels high enough to break *his* neck. "Why?" she asked.

"Because I want to see you again."

"And…" She dragged out the word and kept walking. A slight smile curved the corners of her mouth.

"And I know you want to see me again too," he said, completely without shame. Jade wanted him just like he wanted her; she just had to let herself admit it, let herself fall under the spell Carter was already under.

She stopped. "Okay. I'll have dinner with you." Her face was a conflict of emotions, but softer than it had been for him in a long time. As soft as that evening at her hotel when he'd come over and they'd fallen into bed together. Forgiveness tinged with nostalgia and the possibilities of what could be between them this time around.

Carter only just stopped himself from doing a fist pump. "Good."

"I'm driving, though."

"That's good because I didn't bring my car."

"Hmm." A smile curved her pretty lips. "Your car."

"I know." The Bugatti had dropped enough panties for him to know very well the effect his car had on women. "Maybe you'll let me give you another ride in her some other time."

"You don't have to twist my arm."

The whole time they walked, she walked backward unerringly toward her car like she had both a homing beacon and some sort of backup camera between her and the Aston Martin. And he stalked her, footsteps quiet against the pavement. His pulse thudded wildly in his belly, and lower.

"Good," he said. "It would be a waste to do something so unpleasant, not to mention unproductive, once I'm finally close to you again."

She hummed low in her throat then, at the driver's side door of the car, put her hand on the handle. Jade looked conflicted. Agitated. Determined.

"Don't say things you don't mean, Carter Diallo."

"I never do."

The noise trilled in her throat again. The car opened with a soft chirp and she slipped inside. The passenger side opened and he got in without a second thought. Once he closed the door after himself, he sent a text to Leo.

Heading out but I'll be back later.

Leo replied immediately.

Don't rush back. We got it under control here. Kingsley doesn't even know you're gone. Enjoy your piece of Jade and see you at the wedding tomorrow.

Carter darkened the screen without replying. The jackass.

"So, dinner." He buckled himself in. "How about Sombra y Luz?" He named a pan-Latin restaurant tucked away in a grotto not far from Virginia Key. It was exclusive, private and especially beautiful at night.

"I don't know what that is, but sounds perfect," she said with an unexpected laugh.

He took out his phone to make the last-minute reservation. "I like this side of you."

"You know what? Me too." She started the Aston Martin and roared out of the parking lot.

Jade stopped the car and turned off the engine.

"It looks deserted out here," she said in the sudden silence.

It did seem deserted. Stretched out before them was the rest of the mostly empty parking lot, and beyond it a railing, and beyond that, the ocean. Rippling waves appeared on the dark heave of the sea, white capped under the moonlight. Endless.

The sound of the sea rushed through Carter's ears, hypnotic and low. Except for the half-dozen other cars in the lot with them, it was easy to think nothing was around them but the waist-high wooden railing and the sea below.

"Are you worried I brought you out here for nefarious purposes?" Carter murmured the question as he climbed out of the car.

"No, especially since I drove us here." She closed the driver's side door and dropped the keys in her purse.

Carter stepped around to the front of the car and offered her his arm. "A confident woman. I like that."

Jade rolled her eyes and slipped her arm through his, her smile glinting. "Stop playing around. Where are we going?"

Carter allowed a soft laugh then waved toward the stairs barely visible in the moonlight. "Over there. Come on."

It wasn't until they moved closer to the stairs that Carter could hear it faintly, the sound of low conversation and laughter. Voices speaking in multiple languages—Spanish, English, French, maybe even a dash of Portuguese— coming from somewhere they couldn't see.

Jade looked up at him. "It sounds like ghosts," she said but didn't look scared at all.

"Do you think there are ghosts out here in Miami? Is that why you can't wait to leave?"

Abruptly, her face closed off, tucking away the small amount of happiness that had made her beautiful face even more radiant just seconds before. Carter instantly regretted his words.

He squeezed her arm. "Come. Let's go see."

With her hand in his, he led her to the stone stairs bracketed by an iron railing that had never been allowed to rust. The stairs wound down, slowly curving around the edge of the rocks lower and lower.

Jade looked around; under the moonlight her eyes were wide and intrigued.

"Where are you taking me, Mr. Diallo?"

"I told you, you'll see."

Just as he finished talking, everything came into view. Jade gasped.

The restaurant was nice enough in the day. In a hidden grotto right on the beach, with clear and sparkling blue along the water's edge, it was a very pretty sight. But at night was when the true beauty of Sombra y Luz came into play. The small restaurant used the natural flow of the cliff face to create the illusion of a small sandcastle forming itself from the rocks. Inside, Sombra y Luz was intimate and warm and only had enough space for twenty small tables.

The thirteen tables outside on the beach were the pride of the restaurant, however. Enclosed in their own curtained gazebos and set up on a platform away from the sand and water, the tables were completely private and gave the perfect view of the dark ocean and the lights of boats drifting past.

On a normal day it was hard enough to get a table, but Carter knew someone who owed him a favor, so a table was his, no waiting.

"My father's parents have dinner here sometimes. They used to come for anniversaries but now they eat here whenever they want to have a special evening together."

Jade simply stared. "It's beautiful."

Tonight, Carter was lucky. Bioluminescence was rare in the area, nearly unheard of in this part of the year. But tonight, at the edge of the dark sea and moving up on land, the waves glittered as if they'd trapped the light of the stars and laid them out like a shimmering carpet at their feet.

"I can't believe this place exists," Jade murmured

with awe in her voice. She leaned into Carter as they walked, seeming to barely pay attention to where she put her own feet.

But it was fine, because Carter knew where they were going and guided her feet alongside his own.

They walked along the natural rock path to the entrance of the restaurant where the host stood at the podium with two menus already in hand.

"Mr. Diallo," he said before Carter could introduce himself. "Your table is waiting."

He seated them at the very edge of the restaurant's border where the water threatened to rush up the steps of the little gazebo. The table was already set for two, a small candle in its center burning brightly.

"Your server will be with you in a moment," he said before bowing his head and leaving them alone.

The white curtains surrounding the interior of their gazebo fluttered in the breeze. The single entrance and exit leading straight out to the water invited in the view of the starry waves and the dark ocean beyond it.

Across the table, Jade's expression was still incredulous. Carter mentally patted himself on the back for thinking of this place, and at the last minute. From their conversations in college he remembered that Jade always loved the water.

"Would you like some wine?" he asked, already deciding he would stick to tonic water for the rest of the night. Whatever happened between them, he wanted to be absolutely clearheaded for it.

"Sure." She skimmed the menu but before she could voice a choice, their server appeared.

"I can choose something for you, if you trust me."

The look she gave him was filled with meaning. "Okay," she finally said.

He ordered a Chilean white for her and an Italian soda for himself.

"Thank you," Jade said once the server had disappeared with their order. She looked around her, gleaming brown eyes missing nothing. "When you said dinner I didn't think you were taking me to the edge of the world."

"Do you want me to take you someplace else?" Carter teased.

"Oh God, no. This place is absolutely wonderful."

Their drinks came just then. When the server left, she took a sip of her wine and gave an approving smile. "Thank you."

"My pleasure."

When Carter's mother first told him about this place, he thought it was magic. She'd described the bioluminescence, the food, how special she felt. Even as a kid hearing these stories, Carter had wanted some of that magic for himself. He'd been to the restaurant many times with his siblings and even by himself but he'd never brought a woman, until now.

"Your mother must love it here," Jade said. She was looking out at the ocean, her fingers resting on the lip of the wineglass.

"She does." Carter leaned close, his head nodded toward hers. "Between you and me, I think my father enjoys it just as much as her."

Jade laughed. "I'm sure. They complement each other very well."

"Yes, in work and at home," Carter said, and mentioned the positions they each held in the company for years. "You've gotta admire a couple that can work and live together without getting on each other's nerves."

A wistful look took over Jade's face. "Yeah. That seems like a true test of partnership." She tapped a finger against the rim of her wineglass. "You know, your family surprised me the other day."

"How so?"

"They…they were very welcoming and very sweet to me." Her lips pursed. "It's like they'd been waiting for me or something. It was strange. It was…nice."

Yes, they had been waiting, Carter thought. For him to get his head out of his ass and realize what—and who—he'd been craving all these years. Paxton had made it clear exactly what her agenda was where he and Jade were concerned. Little did she know that it was impossible to get Jade to do anything she didn't want to.

"My family is the very best thing about me," Carter confessed. "Even when I'm weak, they help me feel strong."

Jade fell silent. She turned to look again out to the water. "I wish I had that. When my parents were alive, they only ever made me feel alone."

The sadness in her voice throbbed between them, a painful song Carter felt all the way into his bones. He reached for her hands and drew them between his. He wasn't a guy who talked a lot. Most of what he had to say, he said through actions. But words he felt Jade needed to hear slowly bubbled up in his throat.

"Parents are important, but they don't need to define who you are now. You don't have to feel alone. You don't have to hold on to that hurt they left behind."

Tears glittered in Jade's eyes. "God…" she groaned out, and the unexpected vulnerability of the grown woman he was coming to know again jolted Carter in the most unpleasant of ways. "I wish I could let that pain go," she said.

"At least try. For your own peace of mind."

Jade shook her head and pulled her hands back from Carter's. She took a hurried sip of her wine then rubbed at her eyes.

"I was pregnant." The words spilled out of her in a rush, like she didn't mean to say them. She drew in a breath. "I was pregnant when you left me."

Carter's stomach dropped. "What?" He gripped the edges of the table. "What—what happened?" He stopped suddenly, unable to go on.

"I lost the baby. I lost her." The tears spilled over and slipped down Jade's cheeks. She didn't wipe them away.

A baby? A little girl?

He and Jade had almost been parents. Together. The thought lanced a sharp pain down the center of his chest.

"Jade…?"

It felt like the wind was rushing toward Carter from a long tunnel. The breath stopped in his lungs. His hands twitched helplessly on top of the table. If it affected him like this ten years after, he couldn't even imagine Jade's agony when it had first happened.

"Even though it was my senior year, my parents forced me to leave school when they found out about the baby," Jade continued, her tone flat and calm despite the tears tracking down her face. "They made me feel like I was the lowest form of life. For months, they hounded me, said terrible things to me and kept me trapped in the house with them. Then I lost our baby."

Jade grabbed her half-empty glass of wine and drained it. Then she finished breaking Carter's heart into pieces. She told him how her parents made her feel like less than nothing. And after she'd been left with nothing, no baby in her arms, barely any self-esteem, she packed her few belongings and ran back to the West Coast. At a small college a world away from the prestigious university where she and Carter met, Jade managed to finish her college credits, and built a life and a career despite being on her own. She never spoke to her parents again.

Carter swallowed and the pain of her revelation scraped his throat raw. She'd lost their baby. She'd *lost*. "I...I didn't know any of this, Jade. I'm sorry you had to go through it, and I'm sorry you went through this alone."

"It's in the past." With visibly shaking hands, she wiped the tears from her cheeks. "I shouldn't have brought it up."

"Please, don't dismiss your pain like this. Not to me." Like he was approaching a skittish animal, Carter put his hands in the center of the table, palms out, an offering of hers to take. Or refuse. "It's important for me to know that you went through it and survived."

For a moment, he didn't think she would take his hands. With damp eyes, she looked down at the table, unblinking. Then, she took his hand.

"Can we get out of here?" Her voice broke. "Please."
They left the restaurant before their food came.

Releasing control wasn't something Carter did. Ever.
Too much depended on him keeping his temper. Keeping his wits about him. Staying smart. Staying alert.
That he never gave any thought to just…letting go.

But back in Jade's car, with her hand on the gearshift and her revelation about their child between them, letting go was exactly what he did.

Over ten years ago, he'd left her with a burden he couldn't even fathom. She'd had a child in her belly, cruel parents riding her back and the father of her child off in the wind. No wonder she'd hated him.

"Please, don't feel sorry for me." These were the first words Jade said since they left the restaurant. "That's not what I want."

Carter didn't feel sorry for her. What he felt was anger at himself.

Why hadn't that cowardly kid he'd been found the courage to hunt for Jade once he got back to the university? That one act alone could've saved their baby's life.

Maybe.

He made a sound of frustration and scrubbed a hand across his face. "Dammit all."

A hand landed on his thigh. "It's okay, Carter. Really."

Jade was all composure again, calm and cool while questions burst, one after the other, in his head. Her hand squeezed his thigh and moved back to the gearshift.

They drove on.

Nearly an hour later, they pulled up to a familiar house. The "neutral ground" where he and Jade had had their meeting with Jaxon. Compared to his family's main house where his parents lived, this place was modest. Two stories and white, a fountain in the middle of the circular driveway and a big front yard scented with fruit trees.

A light burned in welcome over the front door. The faint glow from behind the closed windows told of a gentler light source inside the house. But overall, the place looked empty. Desolate even.

He hadn't noticed this the first time he was here.

Jade turned off the car. "If we'd been dating in college, I'd have invited you over here at least once."

But they hadn't been dating in college.

What they'd been doing was flirting around a friendship, then ended up in bed one shocking afternoon.

"And tonight?" Carter opened the car door and climbed out. "Why did you bring me here?"

A motion-sensor-activated light came on in the driveway and all the way around the perimeter of the house.

She paused with a hand on the hood of the car. Slender and deep-golden fingers against the luxe silver of the car. The shape of her gorgeous body glowed in the artificial lights above them. A soft sound. Jade clearing her throat.

"I wish I knew," she said, staring at the house.

Her voice was soft, a little lost, and that revelation of her delicate heart pulled Carter closer with the urge to protect. It was instinctive for him, but with her, more than any another woman outside his family, it swept him away in a tide of action, not just the feeling.

Carter slipped around to the other side of the car and touched her cheek. She was warm. So warm. Her soft skin was like silk under the light brush of the back of his hand. She shivered. And it wasn't because she was nervous.

"Jade. I wish to hell I could change what happened between us before."

Her lips parted but no words came out, just the brush of her sweet breath against his mouth as she looked up at him. Vulnerability swam in her eyes. And it was almost, *almost* like the first—and only—time.

In a rush, he felt swept back to that bright afternoon in his dorm room when she'd walked in, tears sparkling on her cheeks like rain.

"What do you need?" He asked the question and moved even closer, crowding her slender body with the massive bulk of his, lending her his strength. "What can I give you to make some of this pain go away."

A low sob vibrated her throat and she abruptly shoved forward, a quick and forceful motion that mashed their lips together and clanked their teeth. She was throwing herself at him and leaving it all to Carter to sort out everything else. Somehow he knew he'd never get another chance like this one. Not simply her vulnerability, but her being open to letting him fix something, anything for her.

"It's all right, Jade." He calmed her with a hand around the back of her neck. He kissed her mouth, light gentle touches.

"No!" She abruptly turned her head away from him.

"I don't want that." Jade bit his ear, her breath rough and urgent. "Make it hurt."

She clutched at him desperately, hands clawing at him through his sports coat to roughen the caresses and make them more about hurt than comfort. But he'd never hurt her. Not even when she was asking to do it in this way.

Maybe later on they'd explore the option of a mask, rope, something to spank away her fear. But not now.

He forced his gentleness on her. Kissed her mouth, the line of her neck. Her fingers still clawed at him. Under his silk shirt and blazer, the beginnings of scratches burned. But he kissed her sweetly in return.

God, she was soft. Her neck scented with a faintly bitter perfume. The pulse beating madly in her throat.

"Carter, please…" Fingernails dug into the back of his neck and she pushed her hips roughly into his hardness.

It would be so easy to take her like this. Rough and hard against the side of her car. Make her scream in the way she obviously wanted and then tell him to go to hell in the morning, or just after she came.

But no.

Carter's body thrummed with need. His sex was hard and throbbing in his slacks, rampant with mindless desire.

This time with Jade should be slow. It should be good for her. But his body was ravening and eager to have her, and her desperate panting, the curl and press of her woman's body, her sex, against him, wasn't making it any easier.

But there were benefits to being a grown man instead of an overeager boy.

He sank his teeth into her throat. She moaned his name again and moved desperately against him, yanking at her dress and trying to climb him at the same time.

God in heaven!

Growling, Carter grabbed her hands and shoved her toward the car. Her back hit the door with a gentle thud and she cried out, desperate and needy. And so damn gorgeous.

No, he wasn't a kid, but he wasn't a saint either.

He took her mouth. Gave her the rough kiss she wanted. Licked and sucked her tongue and bit her lips until she was a moaning and quivering mess in his arms. Her hips thudded back and forth into the car. She was desperate to have him, to have relief and he was desperate to give her what she needed.

"Love, let me!" He yanked up her dress all the way and shoved aside the thin string of her underwear.

Damn. She was soaking wet.

"Carter!" She sobbed out his name and ground herself against his palm. "More. Please!"

Part of him was very aware of how close the neighbors were. Aware that only a few thin trees shielded the driveway from the street. The car was silver and all anybody had to do was look outside their house to see them. But he didn't give a damn. His woman wanted, and he was damn well going to give it to her.

"Jade, baby." Panting almost as much as she was, he grabbed her knee and hooked it over his hip, baring her soft woman's flesh to his fingers.

Moaning, she threw her head back and licked her lips. Absolutely gorgeous.

"Hold on to something, baby. Just hold on."

Jade reached back, her arms stretched out on both sides of her to grip the top of the car, fingers slipping against the gleaming silver paint. A moan wailed from her lips when he filled her abruptly with two fingers.

"Carter… Oh!" Her hands slipped and squeaked against the roof of the car and she panted and moaned and threw her head back and forth across the roof. The moonlight fell over her like silver raindrops and her damp mouth whispered his name, begged him for more. His sex throbbing fiercely in his pants, Carter gave her the satisfaction of his fingers, three now, buried as deep as he could get into her quivering center.

He thumbed the pearl of her pleasure then fell on her breasts through the dress. Her nipples were hard and thick enough to poke through two layers of cloth. He wet the dress with his tongue and sucked the nipples one after the other into his mouth, loving her deep and firm and hard and fast with his fingers. The weight of their bodies bumped into the car, making a rhythmic thumping motion. The perfect counter to her gasping breaths.

"Oh…" Her breath hitched. "Carter! I lo—" She wailed out, a high, loud sound just before he clamped his mouth over hers and swallowed the noise with a deep kiss.

The kiss grabbed a hold of him in every way. Taking him deeper into the sensation of loving her. And it transformed. Under the autumn moon, it wasn't simply two bodies striving against each other in satisfaction but Carter and Jade, hungry for each other, and finding a brief but still explosive release.

Her body clenched hard around his fingers and she ripped her mouth away from his, panting desperately.

"Carter, oh…" She flailed limply against the roof of the car, gasping in the aftermath of her orgasm.

Reluctantly, Carter pulled his fingers from her humid center. The pulse beat thundered in him and the desire to have her right there in the driveway the way a man needed to claim his woman nearly overcame him. But he clamped a hand down on himself.

"Key," he rasped. "Where is the key to the door?"

She jerked her head toward her purse still sitting in the center console of her car. Jade was limp and gorgeous and satisfied and so damn beautiful. Carter needed to get her inside the house *now* before he embarrassed himself.

He slung her over his shoulder and she grunted with surprise, let out a startled chirp of laughter. But things were long past funny for him. He grabbed her purse, desperately searching for the key as he took her in a fireman's carry toward the door.

"Carter, put me down." As he searched for the key, she was starting to stir again, wriggling on his shoulder and agitating the scent of her sex beneath the thin dress. "You don't have to carry me like some…some prize you won."

Didn't he though?

Her meaty butt jiggled near his face as he carried her toward the house. He gave in to an impulse and slapped it.

Jade yelped, then groaned lowly. The smell of her sex grew even richer.

She was trying to kill him. That was the only explanation.

The sound of keys jingling nearly made him moan out a prayer of thanks then and there.

There!

He grabbed the keys and jabbed them in the lock, wrenched open the door.

A bed. They needed a bed right the hell now.

The thunder of arousal raged, rendering him nearly beyond thought. He sure as hell couldn't talk.

"In there," she moaned, all her resistance to what he was doing suddenly gone. She pointed but he couldn't see, could barely think.

He slammed the door shut and stalked to one of the downstairs rooms he vaguely remembered from the single meeting they'd had there.

Thank Christ!

The bed was big and elegantly made up, like it was waiting just for them. Those sheets were about to get messed up good. With a grunt, he threw her on the bed.

"Oh!" She gasped and her body bounced once in the center of the firm mattress. Before the bed even settled, she pulled her dress off. Then the remnants of her torn panties. The bra he'd only felt under his mouth.

Carter stopped. Because, heavens above, she was beautiful still. But instead of the coltishness of youth, her sleek body was yielding in more places, her breasts bigger, her stomach softer, her hips a lush curve. Her thighs sprawled open on the bed, and it was all he could do not to just jump on top of her and see where they both ended up from there.

Rational. He was *rational*, dammit. He wasn't this guy who'd rip a woman's clothes off and shove into her just to get at his own satisfaction first.

Breathe, Carter. Just breathe.

Yeah, but he made sure to breathe while taking off his clothes.

Sports coat. Button-down shirt. Shoes, belt, slacks, underwear, socks. He wasn't so far gone that he forgot to take off his socks. Or grab a condom from his wallet. Carter rolled on the latex.

"Carter..." She begged so beautifully for him.

And he almost convinced himself it was her desperation that sent him immediately on top of her, mouth opening to the kiss she already lifted her head to give him.

Naked together. At last. Perfect. Nothing better. Not even when they'd done this before.

He panted into her shoulder. "Jade!" The breath gusted desperately through him. "Baby, can I just... I can't wait."

And just like that, she opened her thighs and invited him in. Deep. Deeper.

Wet. Hot. Perfection.

Carter groaned out her name in the burning line of her throat. And immediately began moving inside her. Snapping his hips, the beast in him intent on obliterating its raging need.

But no. No. He was better than this. He wasn't a twenty-year-old kid anymore. He'd learned something over the years he—

Damn… He groaned and gripped her harder.

He grabbed her hips, angled her beneath him and got to work unearthing her next orgasm and his first in what felt like *years*.

"Carter!" She cried out his name like she was saying it for the first time. Sobbing out each time he sought and found that perfect spot inside her.

"Oh my God!" She raked her fingernails down his back, a painful striping, and gripped his rock-hard glutes and began meeting him thrust for thrust.

He felt himself sinking deeper and deeper inside her. It was more than just the physical act of burying his sex into her welcoming heat. Emotions poured from him along with the sweat. Lust, desire, tenderness, Greed

"Jade…you feel amazing. You smell like paradise." He groaned and took her, took them to that place of explosion they both longed to be. The hectic slap of flesh. The desperate moans, the tight grasp of her fingers on his body, in his very heart.

It flashed over Carter then, as sudden as lightning and just as consuming, the truth about himself. About Jade.

He'd never stopped loving her. He dreamt about her every night because he'd never gotten her out of his heart. Out of his system. He may not have been making love to her like a college kid, but his feelings from that time rushed over him like a tidal wave.

Ah!

The bed shook and rocked as he howled out his orgasm and emptied himself into the condom, and she received him with a long and loud scream. The gift of her release.

It took him a long time to recover. He lay on top of her, carefully balancing his weight so he wouldn't crush her while trying to find his breath.

A sharp pain dug into his right butt cheek.

"Off," Jade muttered. "You're hot." But she contradicted her own words when she tightened her legs around his waist, squeezing him with her external and internal muscles. A groan punched its way from his throat.

"Just gimme a...oh damn...a second." Groaning again, he rolled off her and flopped down next to her on his back.

His chest heaved. His arms burned. But he felt absolutely energized. Like he could do anything. When he'd gone with his brothers and Kingsley's friends to the strip club, the last stop on the bachelor party express train, he'd just prepared himself to suffer through it. He never thought in a million years he'd end up in Jade's bed. He'd never had that big of an imagination.

"This was definitely not what I planned," he growled at the high ceiling that had, surprisingly, a fan spinning lazily above them.

"Do you think I did?" Jade rolled over on her side to look at him.

Her gorgeous mouth was reddened and plump, her body gleaming with sweat. His sex twitched. Twenty-year-old Carter would've already had her under him again. Or maybe have her on top this time...

"Nope," he said in answer to her question and willed this thirty-year-old body, that was thickening and getting ready for her again despite its age, to calm the hell down.

Just as he thought to drag the sheet to cover himself, her eyes drifted down his body. They gleamed with amusement.

"Already?"

Please, yes. But he kept that behind his tongue. Kind of. Carter swallowed thickly and tried to cover it with a shrug. He took Jade's hand and was glad when she allowed him to drag it to his thigh, inches away from the thickness of him.

"Is that so hard to believe?"

Her eyebrow arched and he wondered how anyone could manage to look haughty while naked and drenched in postsex sweat.

"They do say seeing is believing and my eyes do work, so..." She twitched her fingers from his grasp and smoothed a hand over his thigh, then an inch to the left.

"Jade..." His belly clenched powerfully and his abs rippled.

It would be so easy, so damn easy to continue this play until they burned the entire night away. So easy. But he was after something else now. Something more. Something for later.

"Jade..."

"Yes, Carter." Her fingers stopped moving and her lips curved up.

"Tomorrow. Come to the wedding with me?"

Her mouth dropped open in surprise.

Chapter 10

She didn't know why she said yes.

But the next day, she sat under the bright afternoon sun in a dress she'd bought just for the wedding, watching Carter stand by his brother as his bride walked down the flower-scattered aisle toward the preacher where they stood.

Idiotic. That was the only reason.

They'd slept together again. And, just like the first time, when she'd rolled away from his magnetic and sweating body, a revelation—or stupidity—came over her. She hadn't learned a damn thing from the disaster of the first time she'd done this. The disaster and the hell she'd been through. At least this time, one of them had been thinking enough to use a condom.

"Oh my God, she's so pretty!" Dee—Paxton—grabbed Jade's hand and leaned close with a big grin.

"I hope I look half as good as she does on my wedding day."

Jade didn't think that would be a problem. Paxton looked gorgeous on a regular day, even when she was pretending to be a regular flake and overall interfering sneak.

A song played over the strategically placed speakers on the wide back lawn overlooking Biscayne Bay. The house belonged to some guy, an investor friend of the family Jade had never heard of, and was the most lush place she'd ever been to. And she'd been to a lot of mansions… The owner and his wife were charming and welcoming though, and if Paxton hadn't pointed them out to Jade, she wouldn't have known they owned the house. They had made the day all about Kingsley and his gorgeous bride.

But she should've been off somewhere, working, not hanging out with Carter's family and watching an ever-after she'd never be part of. Truthfully though, she'd managed to get all her work done, details with Van Tyle wrapped up and dealt with, her contacts in social media and the various interns of the PR firm working overtime to keep details of Van Tyle's foolishness and Jaxon's situation out of the papers and off the internet. So far so good.

So it was fine to take the afternoon off and do something fun. Like watch two people who were obviously head over heels in love with each other get married.

Adah floated down the cobblestoned path like a fairy, delicate and ethereal in the eggshell dress with bright yellow butterflies sewn into it. So gorgeous.

A beauty enough to make anyone jealous. But Jade was only glad for her.

Jade's parents had suffered through their marriage. She'd had enough of seeing that up close even while her father kept telling her his way of being and loving was the proper and right way to be.

But she'd seen more beautiful aspects of love, devotion and commitment here with Carter's family than she'd seen her whole life.

Her eyes burned with sympathetic tears of happiness. Long after she got back to San Diego, she'd remember this day, remember the love here in Miami, like she was part of it.

"Do you take this man…"

Behind Kingsley, Carter stood, tall and big and proud. Like he was protecting their marriage-to-be from any interlopers. Jade shook her head. No. It didn't do her any good to think of him that way. Despite the incredible sex they'd had, he was part of her life that had to stay in the past.

Then why are you at the wedding he invited you to? Why are you with his family?

Annoyed with herself and the voice that had plagued her since she woke up, naked, in the bed her parents had left for her, Jade shook her head and focused on what was happening in front of her.

"I now pronounce you husband and wife," the minister declared. "You may now kiss your spouse."

Kingsley and Adah stared at each other as if they were the only ones who existed in all the world. Jade felt the heat from them radiate and rush through the entire lawn. She sneaked a peek at Paxton. The girl fanned her face with an exaggerated movement of her wrist but a bright smile shaped her lips. Tears of happiness brightened her eyes.

After staring at each other for what seemed like forever, the newly joined couple shared a scorching kiss. The entire lawn burst out in loud applause and wolf whistles.

"Save it for the honeymoon!" someone shouted out.

"All right, now!" came another voice.

The whistles and laughter and well-wishes floated through the bright sunshine, sweeping over Jade and carrying her along with them.

"Come on, let's go congratulate my brother and new sister!" Before she could protest, Paxton grabbed Jade's hand and dragged her through the milling crowd and up to the line of well-wishers. Grinning and dropping the occasional *excuse me!*, she pushed her way through the line and threw her arms around Kingsley and Adah both.

"Finally, huh? Now you can have church-sanctified sex instead of being fornicating heathens all over Miami."

"Pax!" Adah laughed and grabbed Paxton into a rough hug. "You're terrible!"

"And you're part of the family now. Officially!" Paxton squeezed her new sister-in-law then reached back and grabbed Jade's hand.

"You look amazing," Jade said, aware of the receiving line she and Paxton had cut through and trying to make it quick. "I wish you every happiness."

Adah's hug was strong and sincere and scented with a sweet, powdery perfume. Already, she smelled like a faraway place of happiness and endless sunshine. "Soon, it'll be your turn."

What? Jade hugged her back even as she frowned in confusion. Within seconds, she was passed on to Kingsley for a hug from him, then towed away from the front of the line by an excited Paxton. She only had a moment to share a smile with Carter who looked from her to Paxton with amusement glittering in his eyes.

"Weddings are the best!" Paxton said with a grin. "The food is the best part but it's nice seeing the happy couple too." She grabbed Jade's hand again and pulled her along, down the cobblestoned path the bride had come in on and across the lawn, weaving between the beautifully dressed people who'd come to wish the couple well. "Come on. Let's get to the buffet before too many more people get there."

As they walked through the crowd, she chattered on. Saying how happy she was that her brother hadn't insisted on starving the wedding guests until the new couple was ready to sit down for their first toast.

"And that's why my brother is awesome!" Paxton chattered.

They got food from the buffet, which was being tended to by white-suited waiters, and found a table with their names printed neatly on seating cards. At least Paxton found her name. She moved the card for whoever was supposed to be sitting next to her off someplace else and dragged Jade down next to her.

Jade's head spun from being turned here and there by the excited girl. But she was surprised that she didn't mind. It felt good to be wanted. To be welcome.

Paxton babbled on and Jade fell into the rhythm of their conversation with a smile she felt all the way inside.

"I hope our next wedding will have a buffet too." She looked meaningfully at Jade like she was trying to tell her something, but Jade didn't get it. What did she have to do with the next wedding? She wasn't going to be in it. She wasn't even going to be in Florida. Once the job for Diallo Corporation wrapped up, it was back to the West Coast for her.

A dull pain thumped behind her chest at the thought. But she ignored it.

"Pax!" Jaxon appeared out of the crowd, looking handsome and wicked in his groomsman's tuxedo. "I've been looking all over for you." He gave Jade a dismissive glance and she smiled coolly at him. The little bastard.

"It's not like I've been hiding." Paxton frowned at her brother with a bite of food still in her mouth.

"Whatever, I've gotta talk to you," Jaxon said. He obviously wasn't about to go anywhere.

Paxton glared back at him. "Talk, then."

Jaxon gave Jade another look, this one pointed and unmistakable. He wanted to talk to his sister alone. There was something vaguely twitchy about him, uneasy. A pleading look directed briefly at Paxton like he didn't want anyone else to see. It was such an unfamiliar look to Jade, so vulnerable, that she sat frozen in her chair, watching them.

Maybe it was a twin thing.

She stood up, wiping her mouth with the cloth napkin. "I'm going to grab a drink. Would you like something, Paxton?"

"Sure." The young girl looked up gratefully at her. "Anything. Just surprise me."

As dismissive as she was of her brother, she must have sensed his unease too.

With a single squeeze of the girl's shoulder, Jade got up and left the two of them alone. She didn't go far before she saw Carter across the lawn. Her belly tightened at the same time that a familiar warmth rushed through her.

No. Not again.

But the feeling was unmistakable.

Crap.

She clenched her teeth and veered away from him. The bar was just behind him but she headed toward another that was farther away. It was safer that way.

Damn. I knew it was a bad idea to come to this wedding.

"You know I never liked the idea of going public with the company anyway. We should keep it private and in the family."

The words slowed Jade's feet. She turned to see where it was coming from. Two women stood near the water, pretty in their wedding dresses. The man with them looked enough like Carter and Kingsley for Jade to know this was another Diallo.

"Why didn't you vote no, then? You're on the board after all, or did you forget?"

"Don't be an ass. Of course I didn't forget. I just know that's what Mama wants, so I figured why not."

"But it's turning out to be more trouble than it's worth."

"Amen," the other woman muttered.

The corporation's board didn't all agree on the company going public? This was news to Jade. The way Kingsley had presented it, the only person standing in the way of Diallo Corporation going public was Jaxon, and that was only because he was an ass and wouldn't behave himself in public.

Interesting. And problematic.

A few eyes flickered her way. Yes, she must have looked suspicious as hell, standing by herself and apparently staring into space. She forced her legs to move in the direction of the bar. Maybe this was the right time to talk to Carter after all. The business she was there for was more important than any of her uncomfortable feelings.

Of anyone, Carter was sure to understand that. He'd put his duty before his own desires before.

At the bar, Jade ordered a sparkling water with lime for herself and a virgin piña colada for Paxton. Drinks in hand, she was heading back to the table where Paxton and her brother were having their private conversation when her watch vibrated with a notification. Then another. And another. Until her wrist was vibrating continuously. *What the hell?*

Once she found an empty table to unload the drinks, she checked her watch.

They were notifications from the alert she'd set up for Jaxon Diallo's name.

"Damn."

The last was a message from Corrie.

Jaxon Diallo is all over the news, and for nothing good. Now the whole world is convinced it knows all about "Pirate Jax." You need to do damage control ASAP!

What the—

Jade looked up through the crowd to see where Jaxon was talking urgently to his sister. He no longer acted like the same careless bastard she'd met a few weeks ago. Sitting on a chair next to her, he leaned in, desperation all over his face. But he was a little bit too late.

As notification after notification about Jaxon flashed across Jade's phone, she wasn't sure if anything could help them now.

Chapter 11

He couldn't stop looking at her.

Jade in what she obviously thought was a prim dress suitable for a wedding where she wasn't meant to be the center of attraction. The dress was an electric blue and skimmed her figure like water. Clinging here, flowing there, showing off her small, high breasts, the dip of her waist, the hips and thighs he'd caressed and bitten the night before. Maybe it was because he knew what was under the dress. Maybe it was because he'd finally admitted he was in love with her. Again.

Whatever it was, he couldn't take his eyes off her.

During the entire time they'd been at the wedding, he kept her in his sights. Watched her during the ceremony when she was sitting on the groom's side of the aisle. When she'd wandered off with Paxton for food and trouble. And even now, when he was sure she saw him then ran off in the opposite direction.

Even though they'd come to the wedding together. Even though they'd made love one last time before he'd left to come stand up for Kingsley, she was skittish around him. She was avoiding him.

"Carter! I've got to talk to you."

Only years of practice stopped him from straight jumping out of his skin when Jade came at him out of nowhere. One moment, she'd been at the bar grabbing two drinks, and the next she was practically about to tackle him with her empty hands.

Where did the drinks go?

"What's wrong?" Because there was no other reason for her to have that look on her face. Part worry. Part irritation. Part regret.

"The press got a hold of the story about Jaxon."

He cursed. "How bad is it?"

"Bad enough." She swept a quick gaze around the backyard, the wedding decorations, the people, before finally landing on Kingsley and his new wife. "We need to talk. All of us. Right now."

"And by right now, you mean…?"

"Before Kingsley goes on his honeymoon."

His brother and Adah were supposed to leave for Aruba tonight.

Carter cursed again.

"Okay. Let me get everyone together." He turned to get to work but she put a hand on his arm.

"The current corporation board members. Are they all here?"

"Should be. It's family."

"Okay. Get them all together, as well."

What the hell was going on?

But she was off like a shot before he could ask, heading straight to Jaxon who looked like he was begging Paxton for something.

That damn kid…

It didn't take long to do what needed to be done. All the board members and corporation officers in one of the many rooms in the mansion.

Once everyone was together in the opulent room filled with sofas, cozy chairs and a view of the bay, Carter shut the doors and gave Jade the signal to begin.

The room was more suited for an after-brunch get-together than a business meeting, with glasses of champagne, water and other drinks available at the bar and Kingsley, tie loose and draped around his neck, sitting on the burgundy velvet sofa with Adah perched on his lap.

They looked like they were ready for a photo shoot.

The casual groom and his beautiful fairy bride with all her yellow butterflies and the glow of adoration still on her face. But Adah was a businesswoman too and had a look of extreme attention on her countenance even with her arm casually draped over her new husband's neck.

"Thanks for cutting the party short to meet with me," Jade said from the center of the room, immediately jumping into why they were there instead of celebrating Kingsley and Adah's wedding.

Her gaze swept the room. "First of all, sorry for the impromptu business meeting in the middle of this beautiful occasion. Second of all, how many of you want Diallo Corporation to go public?"

Everyone in the room drew a collective breath of surprise.

They didn't need to do this. Everyone agreed long before this. There was no need to have another vote.

"This isn't really necessary, Jade," Carter said. "We agreed to this long before now."

"Let the woman conduct her business, Carter," his father boomed from his cross-armed place by the largest window.

Kingsley only looked at each face in the room, the eight board members and five officers of what had become the life work of Carter's parents. A few of the officers and board members looked uneasily at each other.

"Okay, let me put this another way in case you're too shy to say out loud and up front what you think…"

Shoulders twitched and unease flashed across most of the faces in the room. No one wanted to essentially be called a coward.

"I don't want the company to go public." Carter's sister Adisa spoke up first. "But I know everyone else wants it, so I voted yes." Then she shrugged. "Or I didn't vote no."

Pax raised her hand but spoke up before Jade gave her permission. "I voted no but everyone overruled me."

That was two out of the eight board members. All family except for Nala who was the best friend of Wolfe's wife and practically family anyway.

Carter's own position as chief security officer often felt honorary to him. Yes, he was the fixer and controlled most of the public information about the company and about the family, but he didn't think the title was necessary. Especially since it made him more public than he was comfortable with.

Diallo Corporation going public wasn't something he thought they needed. The family, company or members weren't strapped for cash; his father had always been vocal about *not* having to worry about public shareholders or quarterly reporting. When his mother brought it up last year, it didn't seem necessary, but most of the board and family embraced the idea. So had their chief financial officer. Wanting to focus his attentions on keeping the corporation and his family safe, Carter had gone along with everyone else's wishes. It was simple enough and either decision meant less than nothing to him.

In the lull in the room, he spoke up. "I'm not completely in favor."

"I thought you didn't care," his mother said with a question in her voice. She frowned. "That's what you said before."

"Not caring isn't the same thing as thinking it's a good idea. I said yes, because you seem to want it so badly. But quite frankly, I think it would be more of a hassle than a boon for us."

Conversation rumbled through the room. Carter was hyperaware of Jade pacing back and forth in the room's center, moving between the small gathered groups, obviously eavesdropping on the different conversations, sometimes adding a comment here and there.

"Okay," she said finally to the room at large. "Now that I got that question answered, to add to Carter's point of the IPO offering being a hassle—" she paused until she got everyone's attention and all the small side conversations dried up "—the bigger papers got a hold of Jaxon's history with Nessa Bannon. At least some of it."

From across the room, Jaxon crossed his arms and clenched his jaw. He already knew about this. It was clear as day. Next to him, Paxton pursed her lips and settled a hand on her brother's knee. They both knew.

A wall in the room flickered to life.

Somehow, at the wedding, Jade had gotten her hands on a projector and laptop.

A headline flashed on the wall. Then another. Each more damning than the last.

"Son and Board Member of Diallo Corporation Steals Million-Dollar Idea from Scholarship Student"

"Jaxon Diallo, So-Called Genius, and Thief?"

"Just How Legitimate Is Beauty Giant Diallo Corporation?"

"Working-Class Girl Screwed Over by Rich Diallo Boyfriend When He Steals Her Million-Dollar App"

"Man Linked to Multibillion-Dollar Diallo Corporation Questioned for Intellectual Property Theft"

"The Diallo Corporation: a Den of Thieves?"

The last headline had a photo of the Diallo siblings, all of them good-looking and well dressed, walking into the corporation's downtown Miami building.

"Jesus…" One of the women in the room let out a shocked breath.

Adisa pointed an angry finger. "What the hell did you do, Jaxon?"

"He didn't do anything!" Paxton jumped in immediately to defend her twin.

"He must have done something because… God, this looks so bad."

"Why? Because you don't want your precious IPO offering to go south?"

"No, how about I don't want some poor girl to be screwed out of something that's rightfully hers."

"This girl didn't create a damn thing. She's just mad Jaxon dumped her and didn't set her up for life like she thought he would."

"I'm sure it doesn't help that Jax isn't exactly being nice about this."

"Why the fu—" Jaxon abruptly stopped and took a deep breath. He jumped to his feet and shoved his hands in the pockets of his tuxedo pants. "Why do I have to be nice about this? She and I slept together and it was fine enough." He turned his back on the room and stalked toward their father who watched him from his place by the window. "Months afterward, she wanted it to be more, but I didn't. Our thing stopped being interesting, so I called it off. She went crying to social media and the gullible press that seems to have it out for you, by the way—" Jaxon pointed to Kingsley "—and after that, they decided to make my life hell."

"You mean *our* lives," Adisa muttered.

"By all means, make this about you," Jaxon snarled.

Paxton stood up and went to stand by her brother's side. The twins had been fighting for the last few months. About exactly this, and the joy Jaxon particularly took in pissing people off. When her twin turned his venom on her, Paxton gave as good as she got. But she would give anyone hell who dared to come for Jaxon.

The kid was luckier than he needed to be.

Jade cleared her throat. "Well, I looked into this girl Nessa Bannon and all the friends she's got in her corner all over social media. They're easy enough to discredit with the truth, but we might be looking at a multiheaded beast here. Cut one headline and disgruntled girlfriend down and another set will just rise up to take their place."

Silence rang out in the room. It prickled over Carter's skin and filled the air with uncertainty. Awkwardness. Now was usually the time he volunteered to fix things, use his connections and set things right. He took a breath to offer.

"So what do you want to do?" Jade stood in the center of the room with her arms crossed under her breasts, her feet wide. "Because you have to choose. I can work to make this go away." She gestured to the wall of headlines. "In fact, most of those have already been taken down. But this is only a Band-Aid of a solution. It seems like you all haven't even agreed on the best course of action for the company. Not really." Her eyes met Carter's. "You need to make up your minds where you want to go from here. You can't stay stuck in this place of disagreement."

And that was one thing he could assent to. Grunts of acquiescence sounded around the room. Heads nodded.

"Okay." She clapped her hands once, the sound decisive and loud. A ready-for-battle expression on her face. "I'll step out and you can all make a decision about what to do." She tipped her head toward Kingsley. "I know at least a couple of you have a honeymoon waiting."

With a touch of a button, she stopped the parade of inflammatory images across the wall. Then she stepped toward the locked door.

"You should stay." Carter clenched his jaw and looked around the room to see if anyone disagreed with what he'd just said.

No one did.

"We can decide with you in the room, then we can move forward from here. That way, Kingsley can run off to paradise and not have any of this to worry about while he's gone."

His brother shot him a look of gratitude.

Okay.

"So, Diallos. What are we going to do?"

"Ms. Tremaine." His father spoke up with his booming voice. "Jade. What do *you* think we should do?"

Mouths dropped open around the room. Carter couldn't tell who was most surprised. Him, Jade or his siblings.

Not looking intimidated in the least, Jade tipped her head to acknowledge the question. "Why are you asking me, sir?"

"Because Carter and Kingsley trust you. Even this one here who doesn't have a decent word to say about anyone outside this family." He indicated Jaxon with a flick of his finger. "Plus everything I've heard about you assures me you're levelheaded and you make a decision based on facts, not emotions."

"Okay…" Jade snorted and shook her head. Maybe at a private joke. She turned her head to look at Carter.

Why? He had no idea.

Her gaze was assessing, like she was thinking about more than his father's question.

Was she considering her fee? As soon as he had the thought, Carter dismissed it. Jade was better than that. She'd never choose her fee above doing what was best for the client. Even though if she finished taking care of their mess, she would leave for California. Carter knew that without a doubt.

"Pull the IPO. Don't go through with it."

The room erupted in conversation, shouts, disagreements. But Jade only crossed her arms and kept her eyes on Carter's father, the president of the board of directors and the man who'd made the company what it was.

"Kingsley?" Carter's father asked.

"I agree."

A breath of pure surprise left Carter's throat. His brother had been working on this with the lawyer for months. More than any of the Diallo siblings who had anything to do with the company, he was the one closest to their mother. And while he didn't do what she wanted out of hand, Carter knew it was because of her that Kingsley started the process in the first place.

"Okay," Mr. Diallo said.

"Okay," Kingsley echoed.

And that was that.

Chapter 12

There was no reason left for Jade to stay in Miami.

Outside the window where she stood, a helicopter lifted into the sky. Inside it were Kingsley and his new wife, a new Diallo sister, heading off to their honeymoon in Aruba.

Her job was finished.

The contract between her and Diallo Corporation was terminated. Done.

Most of the wedding guests still remained on the property, dancing and feasting for as long as they wanted. An apparently famous local singer entertained the guests on the stage built for just that purpose and most of the Diallos had scattered, any animosity or incredulity gone once the decision about the IPO was made. They didn't stay mad at each other long at all.

All Jade had to do was leave.

But her feet were stuck.

A sound at the entrance to the solarium brought her attention away from the disappearing helicopter. Paxton stood in the doorway.

"You should stay," the girl said.

"I can't. My job is finished here." And her parents' lawyer agreed to sell the house and throw the money from the sale in with the little bit of cash they left to Jade. She'd already planned to donate it to charity. A home for aged-out former foster kids she recently found out about.

"But surely the job isn't or wasn't all you had here."

Wasn't it?

"It was."

A movement behind Paxton pulled her gaze away. Carter. Of course. She pushed a breath out between her teeth.

"You have much more than that here, Jade," Carter said. His large voice, not quite as booming as his father's but overwhelming enough for her to feel it settle deeply into her bones, filled up the entire sunlit room.

"I don't, Carter. I really don't."

Paxton cleared her throat. "Well, I think I'll let you two…um…talk things out." She turned, briefly squeezed Carter around the waist then dashed away. She closed the door behind her and effectively shut Jade and Carter away from the rest of the house.

"Carter, my home is in San Diego now. You know that."

When they'd first met in Berkeley, they'd thought it was incredible that the two of them were from the same place, the same city, but had managed to meet on the other side of the country. Now the fact of her adopted home being close to three thousand miles away almost made Jade feel grateful. Carter and his family were here. She was far, far away and didn't have to see the beauty of them, where she had no hope of having that for herself.

"Your home is anywhere you want it to be, Jade. Is it just that you don't want to be here? With me?"

"What do you mean 'with you'?"

"I thought I made it clear last night. I want you to stay. I want to try with you what I was too cowardly to offer you the last time."

The last time. Jade bit her lip and turned away from him. The last time they'd seen each other in California, he'd left her with more than heartbreak. Because of what she'd done with him, she lost the last threads of connection she had to her parents. She lost... She just lost.

"No, Carter. There's no way. We have nothing together. And we certainly can't have anything in the future."

"Tell me why. You owe me that much."

That was the last straw. "I don't owe you a damn thing! Especially not to sit around while you run yourself ragged for everyone but yourself."

"What do you mean by that?"

"Do you see yourself? You're running all over the place, tired and hopped up on how you can save your family, but you can't even save yourself!" The anger at how much he'd neglected himself rose up in her. "When was the last time you were home to rest instead of...instead of... I don't know, being out in the streets being Superman?"

"I've been home, Jade. What are you talking about?"

"Anyway. It doesn't matter. None of what you're saying right now matters."

"Don't say that..." He had the nerve to look hurt. "We matter. The future we can have together matters."

Her fingers shivered with cold. She curled them into fists at her sides, trying to stem the tide of words saying everything but the truth.

The truth that she was just plain scared.

Tears burned Jade's eyes.

"But you've never been alone!" she cried.

She shivered and took another step back, shocked at herself for saying those words out loud.

"I'm here, Jade, and if you'll have me, you'll never be alone unless you want to be. And even then, I'd be waiting nearby for you."

God, he was saying all the right things. All the things she'd needed to hear as a scared young woman with her belly full of an unplanned baby. But he was too late. She wasn't that same girl anymore.

She didn't have that much trust. Her parents had burned it out of her and then she'd lost the last of it with her baby girl.

God...just thinking about it brought everything rushing back. The terror of finding out she was pregnant. Her parents' anger and hatred directed at her and the baby. Not even knowing the basic things to do to protect herself during sex much less how to take care of an infant on her own.

So alone.

So desperate.

So terrified.

The tears flooded down Jade's cheeks. "I can't do this with you right now. I…I just can't." Desperate to escape, she pushed past him and ran from the room with tears blurring her vision.

Miraculously, she avoided seeing any of Carter's siblings as she left the house. Outside, she jumped into her car and forced herself to drive slowly, mindful of the tears that wouldn't stop coming.

She was a mess.

She was a wreck.

And it was all Carter's fault.

In the ten years since that afternoon in his room, she'd been turned inside out by her parents, mostly fixed herself, even convinced herself she was completely over him.

She'd turned that teenage love into adult hate. And it had been safe just that way until he'd walked into that office and turned her life upside down.

And now, the adult hate was gone. In its place, a wreck of a woman her parents left behind. Afraid to be abandoned again. Afraid to give in to what Carter offered.

"I can't. I just can't…" she muttered to herself and squeezed the steering wheel. The tears dripped steadily, obscuring her vision.

I need to pull over.

But when she steered to the shoulder and stopped the car, she realized she was in front of her parents' house. Her house now, though not for much longer.

On trembling legs, she climbed out of the car. Inside the house, she stumbled to the room she'd shared with Carter for those passion-filled hours. After he'd left, she'd washed the sheets and remade the bed, then slept there although she still had her hotel room.

This was all she had. This big and empty house. Memories of being isolated from cousins who loved her and friends she'd gone to school with. From everything she'd needed to survive in the world as a woman.

The bed creaked under her weight when she sat down. She toed off her shoes and they clattered against the tile floor. She leaned back against the headboard.

Tomorrow. She would leave tomorrow.

Anything else she had to deal with the lawyer about, they could discuss over the phone. There was nothing but pain for her here.

"Are you just going to mope around in that bed or are you going to give my brother a chance?"

Somehow she wasn't surprised to see Paxton standing in the bedroom's doorway. What did shock her though, was the sight of Jaxon just behind her.

"I don't think I'm Jaxon's type," Jade muttered.

Paxton looked over her shoulder at her brother. "I told you she was a smart-ass. They belong together."

Jaxon turned on a light, then blinked in the sudden brightness. "I wouldn't go planning a whole new wedding yet." He planted himself in the doorway.

A clatter of sound came from the front door. "Where are you guys?" a high and girlish voice called out. "Hey, this house is cool!"

Then a young woman appeared behind Jaxon. She shoved her way into the room, pushing past the twins to plop down on the bed beside Jade. From the familiar set of features and bold way of walking into her house, Jade had to guess this was another Diallo.

They were all still dressed in their wedding clothes.

The young woman, who looked like anywhere from fifteen to twenty-five, examined Jade from head to toe. "You're Jade, huh?"

"I am. And you are…?"

"Alice. The youngest at heart." The girl looked around the room, rubbed the thick cotton sheet between her fingers then over her bare arms. Apparently, she approved of the thread count. "Our brother loves you."

Jaxon spoke up. "She means Carter, by the way."

Jade's heart hiccuped in her chest, then it felt like everything stopped moving. "He does?"

"Jesus on the cross!" Paxton rolled her eyes. "Of course he does. The guy's been gone over you since forever. Please put him out of his misery and just stay here in Miami."

"If you don't, those two will just sit on you until you say yes," Jaxon said. He didn't look like he was invested in the outcome either way.

The sitting wasn't much of a threat. It made Jade think of girls at a slumber party, something she and her cousin Melody had enjoyed doing together until Jade's father stopped…everything. A slumber party with the Diallo girls? No, that wasn't much of a threat at all. Jade had long ago realized she was half in love with Carter's family already.

"Just say you'll stay and give him a chance to make you part of our family," Alice said, quietly insistent. "He's a good man. You have to know that by now."

Part of a family.

Jade's heart thudded hard in her chest. She could

barely hear them speak, the need inside her was so loud. Did they even know what they were offering?

"If you don't stay here, he might leave us," Alice said softly. "We'd rather gain a sister than lose a brother."

Then the doorbell rang. Before Jade could even think of answering it, the door opened. Moments later, Carter walked slowly down the hallway. He took in the scene with little surprise.

"Come on, you guys," he said. "Leave her in peace."

He pushed his way past Jaxon who was still in the doorway. His younger brother lounged sullenly there, looking around the large bedroom as if it had personally pissed him off. "I'm here as moral support for Pax," he muttered to his brother.

"Whatever," his twin said. "You know you don't want her to leave us either."

He muttered something else but this time Jade didn't hear it.

Alice stretched out at the bottom of the bed and pointed her bare feet—she'd immediately abandoned her flats after sitting down—toward Jade's. "We're not done though, Carter," she said. "You can't throw us out yet."

"Actually, I do think you guys are done." He jerked his thumb toward the open door. "Out."

It was sweet. They were all there to protect his heart while he was there to…do what exactly? Jade frowned at the man she loved.

"What are you doing here, Carter?"

He sat down on the other side of the bed, so close that Jade could feel his body heat. "Trying to convince you to stay."

"But that's what *we're* doing. We're already halfway there. If you hadn't come in to muck it up, she'd have moved in with us by now."

Jade felt her mouth twitch in reluctant amusement. "Not quite, Alice."

"You see things your way, and I'll see the truth." She shrugged prettily, then fixed Carter with a serious look. "You've had a million years to convince her to come back to you. We figured it was our turn now."

"They do have a point, you know," Jade said. It had been a long time. Her anger at him and what hadn't happened between them was long gone. Now she was ready for a new chapter in their lives.

"Does that mean you are convinced?"

She wiggled her open hand back and forth. "More or less."

Carter grabbed her hand and tugged her until she fell into his lap with a shriek of surprised laughter.

"Let's go for more instead of less, huh?"

Jade hid her smile in the curve of his shoulder. Already his "less" was more than she'd ever had her entire life. More laughter. More caring. More family.

"Does that mean you *do* love me?" she asked.

He looked down at her, perfectly serious. "I thought that was my line."

"You can both say it, you know," Alice muttered. "It doesn't have to be a thing."

"True." Jade entwined her fingers with Carter's. "I've loved you since sophomore year orientation. How about you?"

"About the same," Carter said. "And because of that…" He wriggled a hand under Jade and into his front pocket. Seconds later, he pulled out a small purple box.

Jade gasped, her heart flying into her throat. "Carter?" Was he really doing this?

"I was going to ask you earlier but I chickened out." He flicked open the box with one hand, keeping the fingers of the other entwined with Jade's.

"Wow! Not bad, brother..." Jaxon whistled.

The engagement ring, a creamy jade stone surrounded by two rings of diamonds, glittered in the light. It was the most beautiful ring she'd ever seen.

Behind her, one of the twins laughed. "How you guys managed to drag this out for ten years, I'll never know. Just say yes to the ring and kiss each other already. I have cake to go eat."

"I have to go tell Mama we're about to have another wedding," Alice said.

Jade couldn't argue with any of those things. And in the end, she couldn't argue because of the warm mouth covering her own. The steady heartbeat pressed to hers. It felt like magic.

Carter lifted his mouth from hers. "So, yes?"

Jade laughed and softened her body against his. "Yes."

He slid the ring on her finger. It fit perfectly.

Loud applause broke out in the room along with the sound of Alice's delighted laughter. Jade didn't even mind Jaxon's mocking golf clap. She was just too happy to care.

At last, she and Carter were back together.

And it would be perfect this time around.

* * * * *

Get 4 FREE REWARDS!

We'll send you 2 FREE Books plus 2 FREE Mystery Gifts.

Harlequin® Desire books feature heroes who have it all: wealth, status, incredible good looks... everything but the right woman.

FREE Value Over **$20**